Secrets of a Hart

~A Novel~

ELIZABETH JAMES

ROMANCE ON THE BOARDWALK
SERIES BOOK #1

Edited by Kathy Krick

DEDICATION

To Sissy and Bobby- You never leave my thoughts and every song brings a memory and a smile. I was blessed to be a part of your lives and know you were an important part of mine.

~with all my love

THANK YOUS:

There are so many people I want to thank but first and foremost, my husband. I love you and I appreciate your letting me continue to follow my dream.

I also want to thank my mom and dad for being the best support a person could have and the rest of my family for being there for me.

I want to thank my "sisters" who I carry in my heart every day. I love y'all and am blessed to have you in my life.

I am also blessed to have a wonderful friend in Kassie Baker who has now endured four books with me and she hasn't killed me yet. Thank you for being here for me. You rock!

I'm so happy to have worked with Kathy Krick on this book as my friend and my editor. Kathy, you're great at what you do and I thank you from the bottom of my heart.

Thank you to Rochelle McGrath for your help in bringing my cover to life. You saw my vision and brought it to life in a beautiful way. I love ya!

To my beta readers, Kassie Baker, Jodi Negri, Maria DeSouza, Becky Nichols and Sharon

Courtney…thank you for keeping my words in the right places and also for giving your awesome feedback. You have been a tremendous help to me and I love each and every one of you!

To my amazing author friends in my FTLOF Authors group who share my love of writing, I thank you. I'm so proud of all of you and am a big fan! Thank you for all of your cross-promotion and support!

To my E. James Street Team: I couldn't ask for a better group of friends and supporters. You are with me every step of the way and I appreciate everything you do.

Prologue

Kendall

I heard the sirens wailing as I came through the woods. My heart beat a little faster as I realized they were headed toward my end of the street. I sped up but stayed close to the edge of the woods so no one would see me. I certainly didn't need to get caught when I should've been at home in bed. Suddenly, I caught a whiff of smoke and could hear the crackle of a fire. As I cleared the tree line, I could see the flames leaping toward the sky, and I instantly felt tears spring to my eyes. It was my house! I could barely breathe as my heart hammered in my chest like thunder. Running toward the house, I saw huge hoses snaking across the lawn all pointed toward the upper bedroom windows. My eyes scanned the crowd of people lined up on the sidewalk, and I saw my neighbors but no one from my family. With legs feeling like lead, I sprinted toward the back door but a fireman, who was rounding the side of the house with an ax thrown across his shoulder, saw me and intercepted my attempt to go in. I screamed but with no sound. Fighting him by scratching and clawing, I managed to break free but soon another strong pair of arms wrapped around me like a vise. Tears streaming down my face, I finally managed to scream out, "My family! They're in there! Help them!" I heard one of the firemen call on his radio to alert the others about possible victims and hearing that word caused me to collapse against the man holding me. There was a buzzing in my ears, my tongue felt tingly, then I spiraled into darkness.

"Noooo!" I cried as I thrashed around in my bed, sweat beading on my forehead, damp sheets tangling around my legs. It was that nightmare again, inspired by my own horrible reality. I could feel every emotion, smell every smell, just as if I was there that night almost five years ago. My heart was pounding, my mouth dry as I lay there panting as if I'd just run the same distance I did that night. With a trembling hand, I wiped my tear-dampened cheeks. Then reaching over, I clicked on the lamp beside my bed to chase away the darkness, for at least a few minutes. After my eyes adjusted to the brightness, I could see the tiny tattoo on my wrist. Laying back against my pillow, I traced it with my finger remembering every moment of pain the day I'd gotten it done. The pain I'd felt on my skin couldn't erase the emptiness in my heart but would be a constant reminder of my loss and guilt. Turning my head, I glanced over at my nightstand and my eyes locked on the simple silver frame that held the only salvageable photo of my family. A fireman had retrieved it from the rubble. It was water-damaged and scorched on the edges but was the most precious thing to me. It was the only physical proof they'd been alive once and that we'd been a happy family.

I'd always been the model child until right before my sixteenth birthday. That was when I fell in love. It wasn't falling in love that changed my life, but it started the chain of events that led to the fire. The object of my undying affection was Tristan O'Neal. Tristan was heartbreakingly beautiful. He towered over me at 6'4" even though I was unusually tall for my age at 5'11". His hair was dark blonde with lighter blonde highlights made by the sun and he wore it short and spiky, an easy style because he played football and loved to surf. He'd been a senior when I was a lowly freshman, and unfortunately, he didn't know I existed. The reason he had no idea who I was? Simple, I was a dork. Tall, gawky, ginger haired and sporting a nose full of freckles that I found unattractive and was always trying to cover up. On the day that I lost my heart, I'd been walking down the hall when I got intentionally shoved by one of the boneheaded football players who seemed to have radar for the weaker kids. As fate would have it, I ended up falling, not so gracefully, into Tristan's arms. Embarrassed beyond belief, I'd looked up to see the most beautiful blue eyes I'd ever seen looking down at me with concern.

"Are you okay?" He'd asked before gently helping me back to my feet. With my face flaming redder than my hair, I'd mumbled something unintelligible and then stumbling away, ran into the bathroom where I proceeded to hyperventilate and bawl my eyes out. My embarrassment was off the charts, but I also couldn't help but relive the phenomenal feeling of being wrapped in his strong arms. And he'd smelled good, so good. He had the sweet smell of soap and shampoo having just freshly showered after gym. I got myself composed, waited in the bathroom until the bell rang and then when the halls were quiet I'd snuck out and found the closest exit door to leave school. I'd gotten caught leaving the grounds by my English teacher, Mrs. Locke and had been taken immediately to the principal who called my parents. When they'd arrived, they talked about how I wasn't a bad kid, and they couldn't possibly understand why I would leave the school. I couldn't bear to explain the real reason I'd been leaving so I just sat there sulking and didn't speak. Since I'd never gotten into trouble before, I was given a warning of suspension and sent home to face whatever punishment my parents felt was appropriate. They were a very passive generation, never raising their voices at either myself or my younger sister, Kelsey. They preferred to be our 'friends' and talk everything out. After a round-table family meeting at the kitchen table, I found myself grounded with all of my electronic privileges taken away to give me "time to reflect on what I'd done". I'd fled their looks of disapproval and my sister's glee at my predicament, ran to my room and threw myself on my bed. With nothing to do, I glanced around my room and spied a paperback that my Aunt Melanie had bought me for my birthday. I settled back on my bed, started reading and soon found myself lost in the story. I enhanced the story by picturing myself as the beautiful countess, Nicola and Tristan as the dashing knight, Christian, who was destined to fall in love with her. I read all night, literally until I couldn't keep my eyes open anymore and fell asleep with the book still clutched in my hands, dreaming of Tristan sweeping me off my feet.

The next morning, I'd eagerly gone to school desperate to see him again. All throughout the day I'd blended in with the crowds hoping to catch a glimpse without him seeing me. Finally, I found a space between the lockers near the gym and flattened myself against the brick wall. People walked by, the hallway buzzing with voices, unfortunately, none of them his. I checked my watch and realized the bell was going to ring any minute. Just about to give up, I thought I was dreaming when I heard his voice. Instantly, my heart started racing, and my mouth went totally dry. He was walking with his brother Ian, who played football also but on the JV squad. Ian was a year ahead of me in school and like Tristan, had no idea I existed. I could feel my palms begin to sweat as they got closer, and suddenly I felt the insane urge to jump out in front of him and thank him for being so nice the day before. It sounded so easy in my head, make it casual, cool. Taking a deep breath, I'd started to take a step forward and that's when I saw that he had his arm around Maria Wright. Maria was blonde, gorgeous and very popular, everything I wasn't. She was the total package: head cheerleader, tall, athletic and above all sweet. Everybody loved her and honestly, who wouldn't? I'd always envied her and sometimes, in the privacy of my bedroom, I styled my hair like hers or put together an outfit copying one she'd worn. The fact that Tristan was interested in her wasn't a surprise at all, but it also meant I had no chance in hell. Feeling like a whipped dog, I'd eased back between the lockers and watched as they walked down the hall. I blinked back my tears, wiped my nose and taking a hitching breath, stepped out of my hiding place.

"Watch where you're going!" I heard as my butt hit the floor. I looked up to see Ian staring down at me.

"What's the hurry, Red?" He asked laughing. Ian was the exact opposite of Tristan in looks and personality. He wasn't quite as tall as Tristan, was thinner and had dark brown hair. The only thing they had in common were the same crystal blue eyes. Now those eyes were focused on me as I scrambled awkwardly to my feet. I was gathering the strength to say something but was roughly pushed out of the way before I could. When I saw who it was, I knew exactly what was going to happen.

"I think you owe her an apology, you big bully." It was my best friend Averi and she was on her tiptoes pointing her index finger in Ian's face. Well, she was in his face as much as she could, being 5 feet tall to his six feet.

He looked down at her and chuckled. "Really? What are you going to do to me, Little Bit. You sure you want to defend your friend? Or maybe we can have some fun instead," he said waggling his eyebrows. Averi quickly drew back her hand to hit him, but I intercepted her arm in mid-swing.

"Let it go, Averi," I said pulling her away. Ian looked her up and down and was about to say something, when we heard one of the kids yell that a teacher was coming so he turned and disappeared. "Thank you," I said looking down at my best friend. She and I were like night and day in our appearance but best friends in our hearts. While I was tall and gangly, she was short and shapely. My flaming red hair was wavy and unruly while hers was thick, straight and as black as night. We'd become best friends in elementary school where she was a year younger than me, but we'd been placed in the same grade. We lived on opposite sides of town but always hung out together during school and always were together for birthday parties.

"Ahem, Miss Hart? Are we having ANOTHER problem today?" I heard the voice, and my stomach clenched. Of all people it was Mrs. Locke, again. "You seem to be involved in a lot of hall disturbances these days."

"No ma'am," I muttered eyes downcast.

She looked me up and down over the reading glasses perched on the end of her nose. "Well, I'm keeping my eye on you. You're on my radar now." With a stern glare, she walked away and as soon as she was out of sight Averi grabbed my arm and dragged me toward our next class.

"So, what was that all about?" She asked as we walked down the crowded hallway. I didn't say anything right away so she stopped me by grabbing the back of my shirt. "Spill," she said with exasperation.

"It's nothing," I said trying to look nonchalant as I looked up at the stain that resembled Marge Simpson on the ceiling tile over the classroom door.

"I'm calling bull on that one," she said giving me a sharp pinch on the arm.

My mouth fell open in shock. "Ouch, that hurt," I said pulling my arm back. "You don't need to know what's going on because there isn't anything going on."

She looked at me and cocked her head to the side. "Do you like him?" She asked scrunching up her nose.

Puzzled, I asked, "You mean Ian O'Neal?" When she nodded, I laughed. "No way!"

She studied me for a moment then her mouth fell open. "Oh my God, it's Tristan?!"

I felt my face flush immediately, but I laughed it off. "Yeah sure, right, it's Tristan." I turned on my heel and walked into the classroom still laughing. She followed me and sat down at the desk beside me giving me the evil eye. Finally, I had to say something. "Averi, it's not anyone. Just let it go."

We never spoke of it again but if I so much as glanced Tristan's way, I felt her watching me. He and Maria ended up dating for the rest of their senior year. I had to endure the torture of watching him kiss her every day at school after he walked her to class and even after the football games. Following graduation, Tristan went off to college in Charlotte, and I was left in our little town of Kure Beach wishing I could see him again. I'd heard around school that Maria and Tristan had gone to different colleges so the thought that they weren't together every day made me feel a little better. One day, a rumor went flying around that she'd cheated on Tristan, and I prayed it was true.

The next year was rough. I'd become the target of a group of bullies and being the daughter of pacifists, I didn't confront them but instead withdrew from everyone who cared about me. My self-confidence plummeted so to cover it up, I began to act out, which threw my parents out of their comfort zone. They were at a loss of what to do with me, and at the same time My one escape from reality was reading. I discovered books that dealt with the same issues I was facing and it was as if my book friends were real. Then I'd started drifting away from my one true friend, Averi, who'd suddenly become one of the popular kids. I fell in with a group who endured the same treatment, and they gave me the protection I needed, almost sheltering me. They were dealing with the same emotions I was and masked their pain with drugs and drinking. I only tried it once then quickly decided it didn't live up to the hype. Despite that, they let me hang out with them but being friends with them put me in some situations that only further distanced me from my parents.

Toward the end of the year, I realized that if I didn't at least make an effort to finish school, I'd never get a decent job, so I made good enough grades to pass. My dream was to graduate and just get away. My parents were so concerned about me that they'd called my grandparents who lived in the foothills of South Carolina. Thinking a change of location would be helpful, my parents encouraged me to go to live with them to finish out my final years of high school. The only part of that idea that appealed to me was that Tristan lived close. I didn't want to leave, instead I stayed at home trying to be patient just wishing for the day I could begin my life totally on my own. I had no idea that right after my seventeenth birthday my wish would come true in the most tragic way.

Chapter 1

Tristan

Pulling up in front of my parent's brightly painted beach house, I shut off the U-Haul truck and sat there for a moment. The house hadn't changed at all since I'd left for Charlotte five years before. The faded replica of the Cape Hatteras lighthouse still sat in the center of a huge flower bed surrounded by a menagerie of garden gnomes. Immediately, I noticed the grass needed cutting and the flower beds were overgrown with weeds, all things Ian should have been taking care of for them. Dad had been diagnosed with cancer and although he'd had some treatments, the doctors had told him and my mom that it wasn't really working. Together, they'd decided to stop the agonizing treatments and allow him some quality of life instead of quantity. When they'd told me of their decision, I knew what I needed to do. I'd packed up right away and headed home leaving my life there behind.

As I climbed down from the truck, I saw my mom coming out the front door waving. "Tristan, come inside for a few minutes before you head to your new place." I took a deep, cleansing breath of the salty ocean air. My parents lived one street back from the ocean, and as I looked over I could see the sea oats waving in the breeze from their front yard. Dad, having been in real estate before his health failed, had been smart buying up the property in front of them after a hurricane had decimated the beach houses. Since the homeowners had had enough and didn't want to rebuild, the lot now remained empty giving them a beautiful view.

I shut the truck door, then walked over to give Mom a peck on the cheek along with a hug. She looked up at me and grinned. "Tristan, your hair is so long!" She reached up and pulled my ponytail and laughed. "You know your dad's going to have something to say about it."

I laughed. "This style is cool, Mom. Don't you think I look like a prince?" I grinned thinking about the comment that I looked like a Disney prince made by my friend Jane's little girl, Jolene.

Mom stepped back and looked at me closely. "Tristan, you've always been a prince to me. I love you no matter how you look."

"But you don't approve?" I asked, wrapping my arm around her again giving her a squeeze.

She seemed to think for a moment, then smiled. "Honestly, no. But I guess that's what the ladies like," she said taking my arm to lead me into the house.

"Well, actually, there was one young lady in particular who liked my long hair but she was just too young for me," I grinned. She looked at me with raised eyebrows and shook her head.

"I don't think I want to know," she said before opening the door. As I walked in, the strong scent of antiseptic hit me in stark contrast to the fresh sea air. My dad was lying in a hospital bed in the front room, signs of how serious his illness had become all over the room. An array of medicine bottles were lined up on the table my mom had set up beside the bed. The room was darkened from the curtains being drawn, and I could hear labored breathing in the bed as I approached. He appeared to be asleep, but as I got closer to the bed, I saw a slight movement as his head turned toward me.

"Hey, Dad," I said taking his hand. He cracked open his eyes for a moment then they closed again. My mom pulled a chair up beside the bed, and I sat down still holding tightly to his hand.

"He's just had some pain medication so bear with him," my mom said quietly as she straightened his covers.

I saw him stir again and his eyes opened then they began blinking rapidly as if to focus. "Tristan," he croaked before clearing his throat. "Son, you need a haircut." Chuckling softly, he said, "Seriously, I'm glad you're here."

Taking a deep breath to compose myself, I looked up at my mom who was wearing a sad smile. "Dad, I'm here to help you both." His hand gently squeezed mine, and then I felt his grip slacken as he'd fallen back asleep.

"It takes a lot out of him to stay awake," my mom explained. "He goes in and out all day. I'm so glad you're here to help us. Ian's always so busy and I really hate to bother him."

I stood and walked away from the bed, so I wouldn't disturb my dad. My mom followed and when we were out of earshot, I said, "Bother him?" I shook my head in disbelief. "He's too busy to cut your grass or take care of things for you? What's he doing? Playing lifeguard and surfer all day. He's doesn't have a responsible bone in his body."

Immediately, my mom bristled. "Tristan, this is just as hard on Ian as it is you. When he does come by, it's painfully obvious that it hurts him to see your dad this way. He's avoiding us because he doesn't want to see his dad in pain. He's always been more sensitive."

I saw tears welling up in her eyes so I backed off. Softening my tone I said, "Yeah, I'm sure it's hard. I'm glad I came back to give him a break." Inside, I was seething. Ian had gotten away with everything throughout his entire life and now, in the time he was most needed, he was letting them down.

She gave me a weak smile and hugged my waist. "Well, thank you for coming back home. It means the world to your dad and me." Tears were threatening to spill onto her cheeks but she took a deep breath, blinked them away and quickly changed the subject. "So, if you need any help with unpacking, let me know."

Shaking my head, I said, "I'll be fine, Mom. The house came mostly furnished so I just have to unpack my personal things. It'll be okay. Plus, I don't have to start work for a week so I'll have time to get organized before then. You take care of Dad and I'll be back to check in later." She walked me to the truck and gave me a quick peck on the cheek. As I drove away, I watched her wave and wipe her eyes on her sleeve. I drove the few blocks to my new place, all the while thinking about what she'd said about Ian. Each and every time I'd talked to him, he'd been vague about what he was actually doing to help at home. Now I knew exactly what he'd been doing, nothing much at all! My cell phone rang, and I groaned when I saw his name displayed. I hesitated before answering, trying to calm myself, afraid I'd say something I'd regret. Taking a deep breath, I answered.

"Hello?" I said a bit abruptly despite my attempt at civility.

Apparently, he didn't catch my tone. "Hey, brother! Mom just called and told me you were here. Need any help with unloading?" He asked eagerly.

This was a surprise. "Uh, yeah that would be great. I should be at my place in about five minutes."

"I'm waiting so hurry up," he said before he hung up. I turned off the main road down a one lane side road that led to my new home. I'd bought the place without actually seeing it in person, instead relying on a virtual tour from a very resourceful real estate agent. I'd sold my condo in Charlotte where I'd been living with no difficulty and had used that money as my down payment on this two bedroom home on the waterway, a reasonable commute from my new job with a local bank. The resignation from my previous job had been a difficult one because I really valued my boss's mentoring. Mr. Davenport had taken me under his wing straight from college and due to his awesome recommendation, I'd be starting my new job at a higher position. It was a major life change but an easy choice. I loved my parents and was more than willing to sacrifice to help them out just as they'd always helped me.

I turned onto the dead-end street my GPS guided me to and saw a motorcycle parked in front of the mailbox of what I recognized as my new home. Ian was sitting on the front step, and he stood giving me a wave as I drove up. I backed the truck into the driveway, and as I was getting out of the cab, Ian came bounding up.

"I'm so glad you're here," he said pulling me into a one-armed hug with the gratuitous manly back slap.

"Hey Ian, I'm really surprised you're here," I said pulling free to walk to the back of the truck to unlock and lift the sliding rear door. As we both pulled the ramp down, he looked inside and whistled.

"Wow, when did you get a Harley?" He said as he walked into the truck to run his hands along the seat of my bike. "Is this a Street Glide?"

"Yeah, I got it about six months ago. I'd intended to do some riding in the mountains and was waiting for the good weather but then ended up coming home. I guess I'll just have to do some rides up the coast." I climbed on the bike and slowly backed it down the ramp. Ian stood watching, a look of envy on his face.

He pointed over to the bike by the mailbox. "Did you see I got a Honda? It's not as nice as yours, and it's, as mom would say a 'crotch rocket', but it gets me where I'm going. My dream is to have a Harley one day."

I chuckled. "Well, if you'd get a decent job, maybe you could," I couldn't resist saying. "Lifeguarding and surf lessons won't get you what you need in this world. Hard work got me this bike and this house."

Ignoring my remark, he said, "Speaking of the house, how many bedrooms does it have?" He peered up at the house then looked back at me.

"Two, why?" I said parking the bike in front of the garage door.

"Just wondering. Um…I really need a place to stay and was wondering if you'd be willing to let me rent a room from you?"

My eyebrows shot up. "Is that why you're so eager to help me unpack?" I couldn't hide the sarcastic tone that crept into my voice.

"No way, I was just wondering. I've been staying with a friend but she's not happy with me right now. You know how women are." Shaking his head, he walked inside the truck, grabbed a box and stood waiting for me to show him where to put it.

I unlocked the garage door and rolled it up. "Yeah, I guess women just can't understand a guy wanting to date two or three ladies at a time. Go figure," I chuckled. "Just stack the stuff in here and I'll unpack a little at a time." With Ian giving me a drop dead look, I rolled the bike into the garage and parked it over to the side making sure it was covered then started grabbing boxes myself. Within an hour, we had everything unloaded and grouped by room in the garage. Surprisingly, Ian worked really hard without complaining, and I felt guilty that he needed a place to stay so I broke down and said, "Hey, if you want to crash here, you can. I have that extra room and the rent would help me out with the mortgage."

"Really?" He broke into a huge grin. "Tristan, you won't regret this, I promise." He reached out to shake my hand. I hesitated but finally, I reached out and gave him a strong handshake then pulled him in for a hug. He pulled away and grinned. "The O'Neal brothers! Back together! I'll bring my stuff over tonight and then we're going to go out and celebrate your coming home. There's a bonfire at Carolina Beach tonight and there'll be lots of people you know. I've been telling everyone about you moving back."

"Ian, I'm really wiped from driving all day. Can't we do this another night?" I really didn't want to dive right into the social scene my first night back.

"Ah, come on! You can come and if you get tired and want to leave, I promise I'll bring you home," he pleaded. "Just have a beer or two and you can come home and crash."

I closed my eyes and rubbed my forehead. "Okay, I'll go for a little while."

Ian gave a fist pump and started toward his motorcycle. "I'm going to take the bike to Mom and Dad's and get the old pickup truck so we can drive on the beach. I'll check on Dad while I'm there." He jumped on the bike, threw on his helmet and with a roar, he was gone. I walked into the house and looked around to see what I was going to need to unpack right away. I saw most of the main furniture items were already in place. It was definitely beach-themed furniture consisting of an abundance of wicker and soft pastels, but everything was in good condition and more than adequate for now. I went upstairs to check out the bedrooms, and since they were about the same size, I chose the one with the view of the ocean. I opened the windows and let the fresh sea breeze in. I was getting ready to open some boxes when my phone rang and I looked at it to see it was Mom.

"Hey, what's up? Everything okay?"

"Yes, sweetie. Your brother was just here and he told us the great news about your staying together. I never did like that girl he was living with. Heather seemed really demanding and I know she was the reason he didn't come by as often. Now, I'm sure with the both of you so close by, it will be such a big help."

"Yeah, I'm sure it was Heather keeping him away," I said shaking my head with a chuckle. For the second time in just a few hours, I knew I had to let it go knowing it would get her all worked up. "Is he on his way back now? I guess I need to get in the shower."

"He left about five minutes ago. You boys be careful tonight. No drinking and driving, okay? Your dad and I worry about you."

Feeling like a teenager again, I laughed. "Okay, Mom. We'll behave."

"Good. You'll call me in the morning then? We usually get up around nine or so."

"I'll do one better," I said peering out the window to see Ian's truck pulling up in front of the house. "I'll bring you breakfast."

"Oh, well that's sweet. We'll see you then." She hung the phone up, and I heard Ian clattering in the front door.

"Yo, Tristan! Where's my room? Are you upstairs?" He yelled up to me.

I grabbed a towel and my shower things and headed to the bathroom. "Yeah, I'm up here. I've put my stuff in the room I'm going to use and you can have the other. I'm going to hop in the shower. Be down in a few."

"Okay, I'll just put the beer on ice while you do that," he said digging through the icemaker.

I jumped in the shower and within a few minutes, I was ready to go. I pulled my hair back in a ponytail and put on a pair of cargo shorts and a surf shirt. I grabbed my ragged docksiders and ran down the stairs. Ian was arranging the beer in the cooler as I walked in. "Wow, you look like you belong again. Glad you didn't come down in a pair of plaid shorts and a polo shirt. You would've had to ride in the back of the truck."

I rolled my eyes and grabbed the now full cooler and headed to the door. "Are you going to stand here all night discussing my clothes or are we going to hit the beach?"

"Whoo hoo!" Ian shouted. "My brother is back!" We climbed into dad's old 4x4 and headed up to Carolina Beach.

Chapter 2

Kendall

"Please come with me!" Averi said throwing herself dramatically across my bed. "There'll be tons of cute guys and you need to get out and enjoy yourself."

I pulled my freshly folded laundry out from under her and rolled my eyes. "Averi, I really don't like beach parties. Usually, there's some stupid college guy who's had way too much to drink throwing himself all over me and I'm really just not into that. You can go without me…you'll be fine. I'm sure some of the other girls will be there."

She sat up and started pouting. "Kendall, you say this every time," she whined. "You need to go. It's time to live, not hide out in your apartment." She fluttered her eyelashes at me. "Pretty please? I promise if you're not having a good time, we'll leave."

I looked at her and felt my resolve slipping. Averi was right, I did need to get out. I needed to live. Lately, the nightmares had been more frequent and more real, and I knew it was because I was under so much stress. The anniversary of the fire was fast approaching, and my anxiety levels had been steadily increasing. I took a deep breath and sighed. "Okay, I'll go. If it'll get you to shut up, I'll go."

Averi broke into a grin, jumped up from the bed, dashed to my closet and started pulling things out for me to wear. "You'd look amazing in this." She pulled out a sleeveless shirt with a brightly colored parrot on the front and splashes of color around the frilly bottom. "Here put this on with some jeans and we'll see how that looks."

Skeptically, I slipped the shirt on and shimmied into my pale blue jeans and spun to give her a good look. "Well, Miss Rain? Do I pass inspection?"

Her eyes glowed and she grinned as she looked me up and down. "Oh yes, Miss Hart. You'll have every guy at the party checking you out."

"Well then I'd better change," I said reaching for the closet door.

"Oh no you don't!" She said grabbing my arm. "You look amazing. I love your tattoos and that shirt shows them off so well."

"Well sadly, the only reason I have these tattoos is because I don't have what I really wish I had." I absently traced the one on my wrist. "I miss them every day, Averi."

She nodded giving me a sad smile. "Sweetie, I know you do. I think it was a beautiful tribute to have their initials put on your wrist and especially the flower on your arm for Kelsey."

I sighed. "It made me forget the pain of losing them while the needle was stinging my skin for just a little while but the loss never goes away."

Averi pulled me into a tight hug. "You're the strongest, most amazing person I've ever known. Look how far you've come in the past five years. Your parents and your sister would be proud of the woman you've become."

Inside, I felt sick to my stomach. My parents would be proud? How could they be? I felt a single tear roll down my cheek, and I quickly wiped it away. Taking a deep breath, I said, "No more tears tonight. Let's go have some fun."

We walked arm in arm out to Averi's electric green Jeep, and we were soon headed to Carolina Beach. Some of our friends had gotten special permission to have a huge bonfire, and the plan was to meet up with several of our classmates and the local surfer crowd. We drove down Canal Drive to the entrance of Freeman Park. Averi pulled her Jeep over, and we hopped out to let some of the air out of the tires to make it easier to drive on the beach. We climbed back in and joined the line of trucks making their way onto the sand. A wildlife officer stopped us to make sure we had our permit to drive on the beach then we slowly eased our way over to the large crowd surrounding a pretty impressive bonfire. We found a place to park away from where the tide might come in and grabbed our blankets and cooler with our Lime-a-ritas chilling inside. I could see Averi scanning the crowd and finally, her eyes lit up as she spied her friends, Stacy and Jennifer, waving frantically to get our attention.

"Hey, Averi! Over here! We saved y'all a spot!" Jennifer said pointing to a big blue tarp they'd spread out to sit on. "Kendall, you can put your blanket on here and it won't get all dirty," she said moving her beach bag over to give us room. "Did you bring some drinks?"

"Most definitely! I brought your favorite along with the plastic margarita glasses too." Within a few minutes, they were cracking open their drinks and sitting cross-legged on the blanket listening to Brantley Gilbert's 'Kick it in the Sticks' blaring from someone's iPod. I sat beside Averi and halfway listened to their conversation as I watched the flames crackle in the giant fire. I became mesmerized, lost in thought until I heard something that snapped me back to reality. "Is that Tristan O'Neal?" I heard someone say.

My head whipped around to look across the crowd, and I felt my heart skip a beat. I knew it was him as soon as my eyes found him. He looked incredible. His hair was longer than it had been in school, and he had it tied back in a ponytail. He was more muscular, if that were even possible. His sleeveless tank hugged his broad chest and by the light of the fire, I could make out the contours of his well-defined biceps. He was still as gorgeous as I'd remembered. Averi turned to look at me and grinned. "It's him," she said nodding as she took a big gulp from her second drink. "Kendall's radar is going off."

I managed to pry my eyes off of him only to find three pairs of eyes fixed on me. Jennifer and Stacy were grinning as well, and I tried to act nonchalant about it.

"Yeah, that's him. So what? Big deal," I said unconvincingly.

"Kendall, we all know you've loved him since ninth grade. You don't have to pretend for us," Averi said poking me in the arm.

"I don't know what you're talking about!" I scoffed. I couldn't believe Averi had said that in front of people I really didn't know all that well. Now aware that I was being watched, I furtively glanced out of the corner of my eye and saw him mingling with the people on the other side of the fire. I could literally feel my heart beating out of my chest. He looked so confident and mature making me feel like the gawky kid he'd caught that day in the hallway. Suddenly, I felt suffocated and I needed to get away. "Averi, can you take me home?"

Averi looked at me like I'd lost my mind. "Seriously? Kendall, don't be mad! And I am NOT taking you home, we just got here!" She emphasized her point by finishing off her drink and popping open another. "I told you I'd take you home but not yet."

With no hope of escape, I kept myself tucked in the shadows with my eyes constantly wandering over to Tristan. He was standing with his brother Ian and one of the surfers who everyone on the beach called Pops. Ian hung out with the surfer crowd which, along with his jobs of giving surf lessons or lifeguarding, helped him meet up with the ladies. Ian had never come into my store, and I doubted he would because my bookstore was not the place to scope out the hot ladies, so I was safe from his attentions. I'd seen him lurking around the boardwalk one morning, but it turned out he was just waiting to harass Averi when she opened her shop. Averi ran a henna shop right next door to mine, and I'd watched with amusement as Ian tried to make a play on her only to be rejected. "Hey, Little Bit," he'd said blocking her way. "You want to take surf lessons? I'll do you for free." Her reply had been short and sweet. "I have a real job, go "do" the beach bunnies," she'd said making air quotes. Head hanging low, he'd walked away like a whipped puppy, and I thought it was ironic that the one girl not falling at his feet was the one who'd been in love with him for years. She'd told me about it one day when we were playing truth or dare. She asked for a truth question, and I asked her if she'd ever had a crush. She'd given me the dirtiest look and then shrugged her shoulders and said, "It's always been Ian." As he'd gotten older, Ian had become a major player with the ladies, and she vowed never to give him any attention because she didn't want to become one of his throw-aways. I'd caught her once or twice watching him surrounded by them, and I'd seen her jaw clench with irritation. When she'd notice me watching, she'd make some comment about him being a jerk, but I could see the hurt in her eyes. Tonight, she seemed to be deliberately ignoring him.

I, however, was spying on Tristan when a pair of jean-clad legs blocked my view. I looked up to see Logan Walker smiling down at me. "Well, well. If it isn't Kendall Hart. You sure are looking sweet tonight, darlin'," he drawled. He squatted down in front of me and offered me a beer. When I made no move to take it, his smile faltered a little but then grew wide again. "So, not a beer kinda girl, huh?" He glanced over at the Lime-a-ritas and nodded. "You girls seem to have your drinks under control. Mind if I sit with you?"

Logan was a decent looking guy but arrogant as hell which lowered his appeal. He worked at a local gym basically handing out towels and giving the ladies "hands-on" fitness advice. Obsessive about his appearance, he spent hours working out in front of the mirrors at the gym and tanning so much he had become orange. He was pretty cocky with the ladies and had the reputation of being a player and thank God, I'd been lucky enough to avoid him. Obviously, my luck had just run out. As I opened my mouth to say no, I was drowned out by two companions shouting out, 'sure' in unison. He sat down right next to me and it was all I could do not to jump up and run to the Jeep. He leaned toward me placing his hand intimately on my thigh. "How's business? Still got old George coming in every day?"

I could tell he'd been drinking and the beer on his breath dropped his hot factor way into the negative numbers. Not wanting to tick him off and cause a scene, I took a deep breath and managed to answer calmly. "Yes, he's there every day."

He lowered his voice so only I could hear him. "Well, I'd be there every day if you gave me personal attention like George gets," he growled. "Everyone says you spoil him. I'd love to be on the receivin' end of some of your attention," he said giving my thigh an obvious squeeze along with an eyebrow waggle.

Suddenly noticing he was getting a little too friendly, fearless Averi reached over and pushed his hand off of me. "Logan, why don't you go find Trisha. Everyone knows you're dating her. She's got it all over Facebook and Twitter. Why are you over here trying to hit on Kendall?"

Frowning, he looked at her like you would a bug before squashing it. "I like to keep my options open and since Trisha didn't come tonight, I thought I'd find someone else to warm my bed." He leered at me. "Apparently, Kendall thinks she's too good for me." Looking over at the other girls sitting near us, he said, "Any of you girls up for a one night stand? I can promise you, I've been told lots of times that I'm worth it." He still happened to slip me a piece of paper with his phone number scrawled on it. The arrogant smirk on his face made me want to slap the crap out of him, but I knew he'd been drinking and that would only make things worse.

I quickly got to my feet. Looking down at him, keeping my voice calm and even I said, "Logan Walker, for years you've looked at me like I was trash and it ends here. You don't need to talk to me, look at me or even think about me for that matter. You are not attractive and I would never have anything to do with you, and if these girls have an ounce of self-respect, I doubt they will either." He furrowed his brows and made a grab at my leg, but I stepped back easily and he fell flat onto the blanket where he promptly passed out. I looked up to see several people were now paying attention to our exchange. A couple of guys who had come with Logan were making their way over to check on him. I also found Tristan's eyes locked on mine, and I panicked that he might come over too.

Averi whispered something to Stacy and then stood to hand me her keys. "Kendall, if you want to go home, I'll get a ride with Stacy."

I looked down at the keys and then back over to Tristan. He now appeared to be making his way over so I grabbed them from Averi's hand and ran across the beach. Reaching the Jeep, I jumped in and slowly made my way across the sand to head back to my little apartment over my store. Once safely inside, I leaned against the door and closed my eyes reflecting on what had happened tonight, and I felt my pulse race again thinking of how intense my reaction to Tristan had been. I'd heard from friends that he was working at a big bank in Charlotte and was very successful. I could only assume he was here visiting his parents because I'd heard his dad was really sick and it made sense he would come home to visit him. I walked to my bedroom and was just about to change for bed when my phone rang. It was Averi.

"What's up?" I asked while kicking my shoes into my closet.

"You missed everything!" She said breathlessly, her words slightly slurred.

"What happened? Are you okay?" I felt a little freaked out.

"Yeah, I'm fine," she said between hiccups. "You missed being within inches of your dream man." I started to protest that he wasn't my dream man but she continued. "Tristan came over to where we were sitting and seemed to be looking for someone. I really think it was you." She started giggling then snorted.

I panicked. "You didn't say anything did you?" My heart was thudding in my chest.

"Psssh, no, of course not. He never asked so we never said. He looked around for a few minutes then he got a call and he and his dumb brother Ian left."

"Well, I don't think he was looking for me but thank you for not saying something…and why do you have to be so mean to Ian?"

"Oh, you know I meant dumb in a good way. And besides, I might be a little tipsy but I would never embarrass you, Kendall. I'm your best friend and always have been. I'm sorry I said what I did in front of Jennifer and Stacy about you being in love with Tristan. I shouldn't have. Please forgive me? I'm your friend and even though you deserted me for a little while, I was still there for you." She sounded so sad and the guilt hit me like a ton of bricks.

"I know. I went through a rough time and I should have never let anything get between us. I missed having you in my life and I'm so glad you got me back on the right road," I confessed.

I heard a sigh then a chuckle. "Well, don't let it happen again! You got me?"

"I got you, babe," I said laughing. "I'm afraid you're stuck with me."

"Good, now get some sleep and I'll see you in the morning." She rambled on, "I'm really glad I didn't drive. I'll get mom to bring me to work. I can tell you right now, I'm gonna need an Espresso and a big blueberry muffin.

"I'll have your order ready when you get there. I love you, Averi…and thank you," I said with a smile.

"God, you're so mushy." She giggled. "I'm just kidding. You know I love you too. Sleep tight, babe."

Hearing the phone disconnect, I threw on my tank top and shorts and fell into bed hopeful I'd have a night without the dreams.

Chapter 3

Tristan

I couldn't get her out of my mind. It was as if a bolt of lightning had struck me on the spot and for a moment I'd been frozen in place. Ian and Hoby were talking about some of the girls dancing together at the bonfire that Ian had a history with, and I really wasn't interested in hearing about his love life. Suddenly, there was a commotion on the other side of the crowd, and I glanced over to see what was happening. Across the blazing bonfire, I locked eyes with the most incredibly beautiful woman I'd ever seen. Seeing her gave me the strangest feeling of déjà vu. By the firelight, I couldn't clearly make out her features, but I could see her hair was fiery red. I held her gaze for only a moment then she quickly turned away. By the look on her face, I could tell she was upset so I decided to check it out. If somebody was hassling her, I wanted to make sure she was okay. I was making my way through the crowd when I felt someone grab my arm. I turned to see my ex-girlfriend Maria standing there with a huge smile on her face.

"Tristan! How are you? It's been a while!" She started to kiss me but instinctively, I took a step back. Her bright smile faded as she realized I wasn't happy to see her.

Maria and I had dated for a year in high school and had planned to continue in a long-distance relationship. I was more than happy to stay true to her while we were apart by staying busy with school and work, but she wasn't. I finally got a break from work one weekend, and I'd gone up to her college to see her as a surprise and after persuading her roommate to give me information, I found her. She was out on a date. I watched from across the room at the restaurant and it was obvious they'd been seeing each other more than this one time. She sat close to him, touching his face intimately and giving him little kisses as they shared their dinner, feeding each other. Funny enough, I thought it would hurt worse but seeing them made me realize that I'd never really felt a deep love for her. If I had, I'd have gone over and pounded the guy but instead, I calmly walked up to the table and stood silently beside them. Thinking I was their server, he glanced up first and was naturally confused because he didn't know who I was but when she looked up, I saw the look of surprise on her face. Her face flushed and she started to speak, but before she could say anything, I'd interrupted her by saying only two words. "Goodbye, Maria." I turned and walked away leaving her to explain who I was to her date.

All these years later, seeing her again, I expected to feel something. Anything. Actually the only thing I felt was irritation that she was keeping me from the gorgeous redhead on the other side of the fire.

"I see you haven't forgiven me," she said pursing her lips. I noticed her hand was still resting on my arm, and I shrugged it off.

"Maria, there's nothing to discuss, nothing to forgive. If you'll excuse me…" I made the move to walk away and felt her hand grip my arm once again, tightly this time.

"Didn't you think of me? Not even once?" She now had a pleading tone in her voice, and I felt my anger rising.

"Well, it was obvious you thought of me when you were dating that other guy. Was I supposed to be spending sleepless nights pining for you while you were out playing games? No, when I walked out of that restaurant, I left all that behind with you."

Once again, I pulled my arm away and as I was walking away, I heard her call out, "If you want me, I'll be around. We were so good together!" There were murmurs from some of the guys around the bonfire when she said that but I just ignored them. I made my way through the crowd to the other side of the bonfire to find the object of my attention wasn't anywhere to be found. I found a passed out drunk laying on the blanket with some girls. I was about to ask one of them if they knew where she'd gone but was interrupted by my cell phone. It was my mom.

"Tristan? I need you to come to the house. Your father's having a bad night and I need your help."

"I'll be right there." I turned around and jogged over to Ian. "Hey, we need to go…Dad needs us."

I saw a look of irritation cross his face but he didn't say anything. He handed his half empty beer to Hoby and we quickly left the bonfire.

As we climbed into the truck, I looked over at his sullen face. "Sorry about this. I guess this happens a lot, huh?"

He sighed. "Yeah, and I try not to let it get to me but it does. Dad's really sick and I can't be around that all the time. It hurts me too much to see him like that."

"Well, it hurts him if you don't go by, Ian. There'll be a day when he won't be there and you're going to regret blowing him off."

"I know. I'm just not perfect, like you," he said as he gave me a sideways glance. I lay my head back on the headrest, exasperated. We rode in silence to the house, and as we arrived, we saw the rescue squad and an ambulance outside. Ian slammed on the brakes as we pulled in the driveway, and we immediately jumped out. My heart was pounding like a jackhammer as we ran to the house. I saw the front door open and a gurney being wheeled out. As I got closer, I was relieved to see it only had some equipment on it. I slowed up to allow the EMT to roll it by and walked in with Ian on my heels. An EMT was talking to my mom, and I could see my dad was wearing oxygen and seemed to be breathing much easier.

"There are my sons," my mom said gesturing toward us as we came in. "Tristan…do you remember Colin Burns? He went to school with you."

I looked at Colin and smiled. "Hey, man! How's it going?" We shook hands as Ian waved at him and went to sit by dad's bed.

"Going pretty good. We've gotten your dad's oxygen levels stabilized. They were pretty low and your mom did the right thing by calling us. He was really struggling to breathe when we got here." He had started packing up his equipment but stopped to check my dad's vital signs once more. "He's doing a lot better now. He'd fought the oxygen thing but it was time. He's had it sitting there but has been refusing to use it. I think he'll be more comfortable if he keeps it on full-time."

"Thanks for taking care of him," I said as I shook his hand again and walked him to the door.

"Not a problem. I'm glad you're back. I'll be seeing you around." He glanced back to Ian and waved. "Hey Ian, I'll see you on the beach!"

Ian raised his hand and nodded.

I watched the ambulance and rescue squad pull away and headed back in to check on mom and dad. Mom was sitting by his bedside holding his hand, and I could see he was smiling. "As usual, you were right," he rasped. "I fought this but it really has helped."

Mom patted his hand. "Honey, you should know by now that I'm always right." She chuckled but I could tell her humor was forced. I glanced up to see Ian looking at me. With a slight nod, he motioned that he wanted to talk to me out of the room.

"I'll be right back," I said squeezing mom's shoulder. I followed Ian out to the back porch. "What's on your mind?" I asked, walking over to lean against the railing.

"I think dad needs to be somewhere they can help him. This is too hard on mom." He was looking at the floor, unable to meet my gaze.

I felt the frustration building and tried not to let it explode. "This is too hard on you, isn't that what you're saying? I keep hearing you, you, you. Why are you so selfish?"

His eyes snapped up and locked on mine. "This isn't about me! I've been here while you've been off to college and living the high life in the big city. I've been stuck here taking care of dad and doing odd jobs because I never know when they're going to call me and need me to come over."

"Is that how you see things? That I abandoned you? Well, if you must know, I've been supporting mom and dad for the last two years since dad's diagnosis. When he had to quit work, they were struggling and I knew I had to help."

His shoulders slumped and within a few moments, he started crying. "Tristan, this is so hard. I don't want him to die." My anger dissolved quickly and I walked over and hugged him, and we stood silently for a few minutes until I heard him take a deep shuddering breath. "Thanks," he said wiping his eyes with the back of his hand. "I know you think I'm just a big screw up but I'm really trying."

I squeezed his shoulder and smiled. "You're not a big screw up and I'll admit I had no idea how bad it was here at home. From now on, you've got help. We just need to support dad's decision to stay here at home and help them in any way we can."

We walked back into the house, and I saw my mom looking at us with raised brows. I gave her a reassuring smile and saw relief on her face. "Everything okay?" She said studying Ian's face.

Ian smiled. "Mom, you know as long as we're all together, we're gonna be just fine."

"Well, your dad's resting comfortably now so you boys go on home and get some sleep. I'll call you if we need you." She rose and stood on her toes to kiss each of our cheeks. "I love you both and am so glad you're here."

Ian and I enveloped her in a group hug, and each gave her a kiss goodnight. As Ian drove us home, my thoughts returned to the gorgeous redhead I'd seen tonight. She'd seemed familiar somehow, but I couldn't quite place why. All I knew was that if she was a local, I was bound to run into her and find out. First thing tomorrow, I was going to do a little sightseeing around town.

Chapter 4

Kendall

I was just pulling the tray of scones out of the oven when I heard the door unlock. "Kendall? It's me, Becky!"

Putting the tray down, I yelled back, "Hey girl, just finishing up some baking. Go ahead and start the coffee and I'll be out in a few minutes!" I heard Becky running the water to start the coffee and I quickly threw a tray of muffins in to bake. As I came out of the kitchen, I heard the bell at the door ring. Without looking I knew who it was. He was right on time. "Good morning George!" I said with a smile.

"Good morning, Kendall…Becky. What's fresh this morning?" George said grabbing a book off the shelf and settling down at a cafe table near the window. He leaned his cane against the table and pulled out his reading glasses.

I smiled as I poured his coffee and added his two sugars and milk. "I've just taken some cranberry scones out. Do you want one of those or would you rather have one of the blueberry muffins I've got baking now?" I carried the cup over to his table and saw he'd chosen a Gina L. Maxwell novel. "Um, George? You know that's a romance book, right?"

He grinned and opened the book. "I'm just looking," he said sipping on his coffee. "I've heard good things about this Gina."

I laughed out loud. "George, I swear you know more about these books than I do sometimes."

"At my age, Kendall, all I can do is read about these things. You ladies can't keep all these steamy books to yourselves!"

I laughed as I patted him on his shoulder. "You're still a young guy, you can't fool us."

"I'll be eighty-three on my next birthday but I'm sure I look much younger, at least eighty-one," he said flipping open the book.

I shook my head and grinned. The doorbell jingled and I saw Averi come in the door yawning and rubbing her eyes. "It's too early for y'all to be so happy. I feel like roadkill this morning."

George wrinkled his nose and gave her a dirty look. "I think I'll pass on the breakfast for now, thanks to Miss Averi's roadkill reference."

Averi slumped down in the chair opposite George. "You know you can't resist one of Kendall's amazing pastries," she said patting his hand. " I'm having a blueberry muffin…if she remembered to bake me some."

"You know I did, and you wanted an Espresso too, right?" I walked over to the counter to start her coffee.

She yawned again and closed her eyes. "Ugh, yes, I need the good stuff this morning. Make it strong."

George clucked his tongue at her. "You're going to regret all that partying one day."

She peeped one eye open at him and grinned. "Are you speaking from experience, George?"

George pursed his lips, rolled his eyes and then nodded. "Yes, I was once a wild kid. When I was a teenager, I hung out with the surfers and we'd get drunk on whiskey if we could get it. Most of the time, we'd steal it from my dad's liquor cabinet and fill the bottle back up with water so he wouldn't know."

Averi's mouth dropped open. "Steal from your daddy? George! I'm shocked!"

"Young lady, you don't fool me. I know you've probably done the same." He reached under her chin and pushed her mouth shut. "I know your generation probably steals worse things."

Averi looked over at me for help, but I shook my head. "You're on your own, kid," I said laughing. "I'll be right back. The oven timer's going off."

By the time I returned with a big tray of steaming hot muffins, Averi was on her second cup of coffee and was looking slightly more human. "Kendall, I'm gonna have to take mine with me. I've got to open the shop. I can see some people are already waiting." She grabbed a napkin, selected a huge blueberry muffin and dashed out the door with a wave. George grabbed one as well and settled back in with his book.

A little while later, George got up to leave but before he did, he put the book back on the shelf and grabbed his cane. "Kendall, I'll see you tomorrow. I'm going to have to read a little more of that book before I decide to buy it." He gave me a wink and made his way out the door and down the boardwalk.

The rest of the morning went by quickly with a flurry of business from people on vacation looking for a good book to read on the beach. Things finally slowed down, and I was able to grab one of the last muffins and a big glass of milk. I sat by the front window and watched the people walk by. I saw a couple of young women heading to Averi's store, and I laughed to myself, knowing their intentions. They all did the same thing on vacation. They got matching henna designs. Averi's store was popular and she fit right in with the younger crowd. She kept her hair dyed in the popular ombre style with her naturally dark hair tipped with purple ends and she usually had some of her own henna designs on her hands to demonstrate. I was so lost in thought that I didn't hear the doorbell ring but when I heard a familiar voice, one I didn't want to hear, I was chilled to the bone.

"Good afternoon, Kendall. Just thought I'd drop by and say hello." It was Sebastian Cole. He and I had once been really close friends but that was all in the past. Now my skin crawled whenever I saw him. This was not a welcome visit.

"Sebastian. What can I do for you?" I asked icily.

He ran his hand through his spiked black hair. "Well, so far you're doing it and I want it to stay that way. You're a smart girl and I know you'll behave but I just need to come by once in a while and remind you." He sat down in the chair across from me, and I felt a knot form in my stomach. I started to stand but he grabbed my arm and pulled me back down into the chair. He reached across the table and brushed the hair from my eyes, and I couldn't hide my flinch. "You've always been my biggest regret, Kendall. I wish it had never happened but sometimes fate deals us a hand we don't expect…or want. I know you're doing okay here and I got a job so we're all set. Model citizens. No need to rock the boat."

I looked at him with disgust. Keeping my voice low to not attract the attention of the others in the store, I said, "You think my life is okay? It's not." I choked back a sob. "I live with the guilt every day and I have nightmares almost every night."

He leaned back in his chair and chuckled. "Well, then I still have some control over you. I'm glad to hear that." Suddenly, he leaned forward and gripped my arm tightly. "The day you think you can ease your conscience and tell everything you know will be your last. You of all people should know what I'm capable of."

"Is everything okay, Kendall?" I heard Becky ask from the back of the store.

I took a deep breath before answering. "Yes, everything's fine." Sebastian grinned and stroked my arm seductively with his thumb making little circles on my skin. I felt nothing but revulsion.

His voice was low as he said, "You could make this arrangement even sweeter, Kendall. We don't have to be enemies. We could be good together." I saw him lick his lips, and I closed my eyes and slowly pulled my arm away.

"That will never happen. Now, leave me alone. I'm not going to say or do anything. You don't have to watch over me. Our discussion is over. You can leave now." I stood to emphasize he'd worn out his welcome.

With a disappointed look, he stood and unexpectedly wrapped his arms around me tightly. To anyone watching it would appear we were hugging like old friends. He whispered in my ear, "I'll be watching you, gorgeous."

He let go and as he did, he pushed me back. I almost lost my balance but was lucky enough to grip the back of the chair to keep from falling. With a final sneer, he opened the door just as Averi was coming in. He held the door open and stepped aside so she could come in. "Good afternoon," he said eyeing her up and down. With a final exaggerated wink, he was gone.

Averi watched him leave then turned to me. "You okay? What was that all about?" I couldn't tell her. I'd been keeping this secret for years, and I believed Sebastian's threats and was not about to "rock the boat" as he put it.

"Unhappy customer," I simply said as I gathered my napkin and empty milk glass.

"Kendall Grace...you can't fool me. I know who he is. What was Sebastian Cole doing here? You look like you've seen a ghost. Did he upset you?"

I could feel tears welling up in my eyes, but I quickly turned my head to look out the picture window. Nervously laughing I said, "No, it's nothing. He has it in his head that he likes me and just comes on strong and can't get the hint. Maybe one day he'll figure it out." I turned and quickly walked to the kitchen. I could tell Averi wasn't going to let it go, and I was right. She followed me into the kitchen and stood right in front of me.

"We've been friends too long to have secrets. I don't know what's going on but I want you to know that whatever it is, you can tell me." She didn't budge, and I was forced to look at her.

"I can't." I took a deep breath. "Just let it go." The bell signaled the door opening and another customer coming in. "I've got to get back to work, Becky's gone to her night class and I'm here alone."

Averi stepped aside and let me pass but I could sense this wasn't over. "I've got some afternoon appointments but I'll be free after that. When you're ready to talk, I'll be here to listen." She walked out the back door slamming it as she left. I stopped to grab a tray of fresh scones and walked out front. "May I help—"

I froze. It was Tristan.

I felt my mouth flop open, and as I saw him smile, I popped it shut and tried to act normally. My heart was hammering in my chest, and I had to force myself to breathe so acting naturally took a lot of effort.

His beautiful blue eyes were locked on mine, and I realized this was the first time I'd been this close to him since that day in school. I stood there mutely for a moment then found my voice. "May I help you?"

His voice was deeper and more mature and I felt goosebumps hearing it after all these years. "Yes, I'd like an iced coffee and a half dozen of those gorgeous scones you're holding, if you don't mind."

I looked down at the tray in my hands then back up and nodded. Setting the tray down, I quickly rang up his purchase and as he handed the money to me, our hands touched. I felt a jolt of electricity and looked up in surprise only to find him looking at me with a startled look as well. "Um, you can go find a seat and I'll bring your order to you," I mumbled absently rubbing my hand.

He nodded and looked at me curiously for a moment then headed to the table by the window. The only remaining customer got up and waved as they left and it was just Tristan and I. After I'd made his coffee and placed the nicest scones in a box, I carried them out to his table and saw he'd picked up a paperback that I'd been leafing through. Looking up, he smiled, glanced at my name tag and said, "Kendall? Would you like to join me?" He gestured toward the chair across from him.

"Well, I really need to keep an eye on things," I said, shuffling my feet nervously. He didn't seem to recognize me, and I really wanted to keep it that way.

He looked around the empty store and chuckled. "I promise if things get busy, I'll let you go. For now, I'd like you to join me. I'm Tristan…Tristan O'Neal." He held out his hand and after a moment's hesitation, I took it. Again, I felt that jolt as we touched and the tingle lingered even after I pulled my hand away. The rumble of his deep voice made me breathless and with my heart pounding, I sat down across from him. I looked down at the table and could feel his eyes on me. Finally, I got the courage to look at him eye to eye. I swallowed hard and waited to see if he'd figure out who I was. He studied me for a moment then finally spoke. "I saw you last night...at the bonfire."

I wasn't expecting that. I'd seen him looking at me but figured I was just another face in the sea of people around the fire. I didn't want him to know I'd seen him, so I acted surprised. "You were there? I think I would've remembered seeing you."

"I actually was on my way over to talk to you when you disappeared. I have to ask, did someone upset you? You left pretty quickly." He took a sip of his coffee and as I watched him lick his lips, I unconsciously licked my own.

Recovering quickly, I said, "Well, it wasn't anything I couldn't handle." I shrugged. "That guy is always scamming on someone and last night he chose me. I set him straight and decided it would be better if I left so I came home."

He nodded slowly still studying my face. I glanced around avoiding his gaze but I kept being drawn back to those beautiful crystal blue eyes. "I feel like I know you," he said. "It's so funny, I mean, how could I know you? I've been gone for a few years and there's no way I would've forgotten someone as beautiful as you. Did you grow up around here?"

My face flushed crimson, and I shook my head. I couldn't let him know I was the dork from high school. "Somewhere close by," I finally answered.

He studied me for a moment longer, then continued. "Well, I went to high school here and ended up moving to Charlotte for college and then to Asheville for my job. I've just moved back here. My dad's really sick and my parents need my brother and me to help them out." I nodded slowly letting him continue. The less I said the better.

I could see the pain and worry on his face. "I hope your dad's going to be okay," I said sincerely.

He leaned back in his chair and took a deep breath. "I'll be honest with you, I don't think he will. He has cancer and it's pretty advanced. My parents decided to stop the treatments to give him some quality of life but he's not giving up. As long as he's fighting, I will too.

But I have to be realistic and prepared for the worst. I just saw them this morning for breakfast and could tell he's declined just since yesterday."

I felt tears welling up in my eyes not only for his parents but for my own family. "I'm sure your parents appreciate the sacrifices you've made for them. Spend every moment you can with those you love. Those memories are priceless."

He nodded thoughtfully. "Yes, I agree and they both fought me about moving back. They knew I had a life and a great job there and they didn't want me to give it all up."

"It had to be hard to leave your friends," I said, crossing my fingers under the table that a girlfriend wasn't part of his life now.

"I had some friends but mostly kept to myself. I'm not the partying kind of guy and so I spent a lot of Saturday nights in front of my tv and also I love to read."

I smiled thinking of my small circle of friends. "I'm the same way. I have a best friend, Averi, who works at the henna shop next door and a few friends I see now and then but that's it. I live in an apartment upstairs so I'm either at work or at home. It was totally out of character for me to go to a bonfire and truthfully I didn't want to go."

He leaned toward me and lightly brushed the back of my hand with his finger. "I'm glad you did." My eyes met his and I shyly smiled. "Kendall, would you like to have dinner with me sometime? I'd love to get to know you better."

Fear suddenly gripped me like someone had doused me with a cold bucket of water and I jumped up from the chair. "I'd really love to but I'm going through some stuff right now and I wouldn't make good company. Thank you for asking me though." I scurried back to the kitchen and once inside I leaned against the wall taking deep breaths trying to calm myself. Tristan O'Neal asked me out! I had to be dreaming. This was what I'd always wished for and now it had actually happened. But I'd said no. What was I thinking? He must think I'm a total loser. I leaned around the door to take a peek at him and saw him drop something down on the table and head out the door. As I heard the door close, I banged the back of my head against the wall. "Kendall, you fool!" I said out loud. I waited a few moments then went out to clean up the table. I looked down and saw he'd left a note on his napkin. I picked it up and read: *If you change your mind, here's my number.* I held the napkin close to my chest and sank down into the chair. My heart was telling me to call him but my head was telling me that my life was too complicated to invite him in. I glanced at the napkin once more then folded it and put it in my pocket. How could fate be so cruel to give me what I'd always wanted when there was no way in the world I could have it.

Chapter 5

Tristan

What unbelievable luck! I'd had her on my mind all night and this morning. Lured by the amazing smell of fresh coffee, I'd stumbled across my mysterious blue-eyed redhead. She'd seemed surprised when she first saw me, but that couldn't have been the case. We'd never met before. When our hands touched, I'd felt a spark, and I could see it affected her as well. She was totally breathtaking in the light of day. After she brought my order to the table, I tried to make small talk to make her feel comfortable and also get to know who she was. Spending just those few moments with her made me want more but when I made the bold move to ask her to dinner, she'd immediately pulled back. I needed to see her again. As I got up to leave, I took a napkin and jotted my number down hoping she'd see it and give me a chance. I closed the door of the store and turned to walk down the boardwalk. I was passing the henna shop and remembered that Kendall said her best friend, Averi, worked there. I decided to see if I could get some information from her that would help me persuade Kendall to go out with me. I entered the shop and saw two young women wearing bikinis standing around a photo book and they looked up at me and started whispering and giggling.

"If you want the henna done today, you'd better pick something out now because I close in an hour," a young woman, who I assumed was Averi, with jet black hair tipped with purple, said as she came from the back of the store. She glanced over at me and her mouth fell open reminiscent of the way Kendall's did when she saw me. She quickly recovered, gave me a forced hello then turned her attention to the girls.

"Natalie and I want matching ones!" Said one of the young women. "Do you have time to do us both?"

Averi glanced at the design in the book and appeared to calculate the time needed. "Yeah, I can do them both but we need to get started." She turned to look at me. "Are you interested in getting one too?" She gave me a mischievous grin.

"No, but if you're Averi, I was actually wondering if I could talk to you. I'm willing to wait until you're finished."

She shrugged her shoulders. "Yeah, that's me. If you want to wait, whatever...it'll be about forty-five minutes. Is that okay?"

"Sure, I'm actually curious about how this is done. Can I watch?" The two young women blushed and giggled when I said that.

Averi rolled her eyes at them and nodded. "As long as it's okay with them." They both nodded vigorously in agreement and Averi indicated to a nearby chair. "Who's first?"

Natalie motioned to her friend. "Alicia, you go first. I'm scared it's going to hurt." They held each other's hands nervously.

"It doesn't hurt," Averi said getting her supplies organized. "There aren't any needles like a real tattoo. I use a plastic tip that applies the henna paste to your skin. I also don't use black henna which can cause allergic reactions. My designs will be a little lighter but you won't be carrying blisters around on vacation."

Alicia took a deep breath and sat down in the chair. "I want it on my right shoulder. I like the flower," she said pointing to a page in the book.

Averi took an alcohol swab and cleaned the area then began applying the paste in an intricate pattern that eventually became an exact replica of the picture. It only took about ten minutes and I watched fascinated. "Okay, you're done. Now, don't touch anything or you'll end up with a smeared mess for two weeks."

Alicia got up and looked in the mirror. "It's beautiful! Natalie, it didn't hurt a bit."

Grinning, Natalie sat in the chair and the same process was repeated. Once she was satisfied with her design, they admired each other's and then begged me to take a picture of them with their phones, which I did. Averi told them how to take care of them and they left still admiring each other.

Averi washed her hands and put them on her hips and said, "So what do you want Mr….?"

I could tell she was a pint-sized force to be reckoned with so I gave her my most charming smile. "O'Neal. Tristan O'Neal. I just met your friend Kendall and I'm really interested in taking her out but she pretty much blew me off. I need some help."

She appeared amused. "So, you want ME to help YOU persuade Kendall to go out with you." She muttered something under her breath and chuckled.

"You find this funny?" I said with surprise.

She cocked one eyebrow. "Well, yes and no. Yes, because I find it hard to believe that you would have a hard time getting ANYONE to go out with you. And no, because I think it's incredible that she said no." She shook her head and started closing up her cash register. "What do you want to know?"

"Well, I'd like to know if it's just me or if she's just not into dating anyone right now. She said her life was complicated so I wondered if she was seeing someone," I said leaning against the counter.

She turned to look at me and smiled. "She is VERY single and I can honestly say, it's not you. I'm not sure if she's afraid or what it is. I've found her to be very secretive lately myself and I've known her most of my life. The only advice I can give you is not to give up. I know her type and you are MOST definitely her type," she said laughing.

"Averi, can you tell me something that she really likes so I can at least make an impression?"

She thought for a moment then got a sly smile. "Well, her favorite flowers are lilies. That'll give you somewhere to start. I'm pretty sure if you get her some, she'll probably cave and at least go to dinner with you. Her favorite restaurant is Oceanic and she loves seafood. The rest is up to you."

I smiled and held open my arms. "Thank you so much! Can I give you a hug? I've at least got some hope now."

She hesitated then grinned. "Sure, why not."

I hugged her picking her up in the process. "I owe you big time, Averi."

"I'll remember that. I just may call in that favor one day," she said still grinning. I set her back down and with a grin, opened the door and left.

I went straight to the closest florist. The woman inside was just about to turn over the OPEN sign when I came running up to the door. "Please, I know you're closing but I know what I want and I promise you I'll pay extra for your time."

She looked at my desperate face and laughed. "Forget a birthday or anniversary?"

Trying to catch my breath I managed to say, "Trying to get a date."

The woman looked at me with surprise. "You? I can't see how you'd need anything to get a date."

I shook my head and chuckled. "That's the second time I've heard something like that today. I'm starting to feel pretty good about myself."

Going behind the counter she said, "What are you looking for? Roses?"

"No, I want lilies. The biggest and most beautiful you have. I want them delivered to Kendall…oh, crap…I don't know her last name. She owns the coffee shop on the boardwalk."

The woman's eyebrows raised. "Oh, you mean Kendall Hart. I know her. Such a sweet girl. Such a tragic life."

Puzzled, I asked, "Tragic?"

The woman was busily writing the address details down and answered, "Yes, I don't know the details but I've heard a few years ago, she had something terrible happen to her."

Now I was really intrigued. "You don't know any more than that?"

"No, I'm sorry. We moved here a couple of years ago and all I've gotten is some gossip here and there." I handed her my credit card and she rang up my order. "Your flowers will be delivered tomorrow around midday. Here's a card that you can write a message on."

I took the card and a pen and wrote, *You've captured my interest, please say I've captured yours. Dinner? I hope you kept my number…*

The woman took my card and attached it to my order. "Good luck, Mr. O'Neal. Kendall's a real beauty, inside and out."

I nodded. "I have to agree. Thank you again for staying open for me. This really means a lot."

She smiled and walked me to the door. "I have a feeling I'll be seeing a lot of you. I give discounts for repeat customers," she said giving me a wink. "And my name's Judy. Make sure to ask for me."

I walked out with a satisfied grin knowing that tomorrow, Kendall was going to get a wonderful surprise.

I called my parents to check in and all was well. As I drove up to the house, I saw Ian's bike sitting out front of the house. I went in and saw him stretched out on the couch texting on his phone. "Hey, brother," he said looking up. "I knew you'd be hungry so I ordered pizza for dinner but I'm a little short on cash so can you get it this time? I promise I'll get it next time."

I threw my keys down on the counter and grabbed a beer from the fridge. I noticed that Ian had been helping himself to the groceries and with a sinking feeling, realized that I now had a dependant. I sighed and got some money out of my wallet to pay for the pizza. I looked at him lying there and a pang of guilt hit me. He was my brother and no matter how aggravating he could be, I loved him. "So, did you work today?"

He glanced up from his phone for a moment. "Um, not really. There were some really good waves today so I went surfing with some of the guys. You remember Hoby? He was helping me with some of my moves. He was a pro surfer and he's really good at it. I'd love to go to Hawaii and hit the really big waves but for now, I'll just stick with working on my technique. I'm gonna have to save up for that kind of trip." He went back to texting and when the doorbell rang, he glanced up at me. "That's probably the pizza guy." He never moved from the couch. Rolling my eyes, I went to the door.

I opened the door expecting our dinner but instead saw a young woman standing there in a tube top and daisy dukes. "Hey, is Ian home?" I glanced back and saw he'd vanished from the couch.

I hesitated and finally said, "Wait here, let me see. I just got home…um, I'm sorry, I don't know your name."

"Danielle…my name's Danielle. I met Ian on the beach today and he told me this was his house. You must be his brother Tristan. It's so nice of Ian to let you stay with him."

My eyes grew wide. "Me stay with him? Uh, sure." Shaking my head, I walked back toward the guest room. I could hear him shuffling around in the room so I quietly knocked. "You here?"

"No," he whispered. "Tell her I'm at work."

"You owe me little brother." I walked back out shaking my head. "Sorry, Danielle. He's at work. He won't be back until late. I'm sure he'll call you tomorrow sometime."

She stood there for a moment then looked me up and down. "So, are you single? I was in the mood to play…"

"No, I'm sorry. I'm seeing someone," I answered quickly. I wasn't really lying because I had seen Kendall today and hopefully would see her again soon.

She pouted. "Bummer. Oh well, if you're up for a good time, give me a call." She waggled her eyebrows at me and licked her lips. I shut the door and shook my head. I saw Ian come creeping out of the bedroom.

"Did she leave?" He whispered. He walked over to peek out of the blinds.

"Yes, and I have to thank you for being so generous to let me stay here with you. I don't know what I would've done if you hadn't taken me in," I said sarcastically.

I saw him cringe. "Did she tell you that? I can explain." His explanation was interrupted by the doorbell. Shaking my head, I went to answer it and found the pizza guy holding not one but two extra-large pizzas. I looked at Ian who grinned and rubbed his stomach so I paid the guy and put the pizza down on the counter. The next thing I knew, Ian had the box open and was eating the pizza right out of the box. I grabbed some paper plates and handed one to him along with a napkin. He looked at me and laughed. "Thanks, Mom."

"Ian, you're lucky I'm not her. Now, what's the deal with the girl." I took a bite of pizza which was actually really good.

Holding up a finger to tell me to wait, Ian finished chewing the huge bite he'd just taken. He chugged some of my beer with it so I reached in the fridge and grabbed a fresh one for me. Finally, he spoke. "Okay, I was down on the beach today with Jake and Hunter. Pops was in the water showing us some really cool moves when a girl I know from lifeguarding lessons came walking up with her friends. My friend Luke introduced me to Danielle and Heather and Danielle started hanging on me. She asked where I lived and the guys started laughing because they thought I was staying with mom and dad so I told her that I had a house and that you were staying with me."

I shook my head. "Well, I'll let it slide this time," I said, popping him on the back of his head. "Just don't tell them where you live, you idiot. I'm not going to have women in and out of here, especially when I'm not at home."

He shrugged. "Sorry, man. I'll respect your space from now on. So, what did you do today?"

I really didn't want to tell him about Kendall so I dodged that by telling him I wandered on the boardwalk and ventured into the henna shop.

"You were in Averi's shop?" He asked, eyes wide.

"Yeah, you know her?"

"Sure, she went to school with us. I don't like her and I don't think she likes me." He went back to eating but it was pretty obvious he was lying. His body language had changed instantly and he seemed agitated.

"Well, I talked to her and watched her do a henna stain. She's really something." I took a bite of my pizza and watched him closely.

"Yeah, she's different. Every time I try to talk to her, she blows me off. I'm not wasting my time with her." The words coming out of his mouth didn't mirror the look in his eyes. Yep, baby brother had a crush on the pint-sized powerhouse. It was written all over his face.

"Well, that's a shame, I think she's gorgeous and really sweet." I was baiting him and it felt good.

Averting his eyes, he shifted on his feet as he took another bite of pizza. "I'd stay away from her Tristan. She's not your type anyway." I could see his jaw had tightened as he chewed his food slowly and deliberately.

I decided to let him off the hook. "Well, it seems like she'd be someone cool to be friends and hang out with."

"Yeah," he agreed. "Too bad she won't talk to me." He really seemed to be bothered by it.

I finished off my beer and the last bite of my pizza then started cleaning up. Ian hesitated as if he wanted to say something else but instead slightly shook his head, grabbed his phone and started texting again.

"Well, I'm going to my room to watch tv for a while then I'm headed to bed. I'm starting my new job in the morning and since it's in Wilmington, it'll take me at least thirty minutes to get there." Ian nodded but never looked up from his phone. "Goodnight."

Ian mumbled something that sounded like goodnight. I went to my room, laid out my clothes for the next morning, watched part of a movie then headed to bed. As I lay there, my thoughts were on Kendall. She was breathtakingly beautiful, but it was obvious to me that she had no idea just how gorgeous she was. I was determined to find out more about her, and I couldn't wait to see if my flowers would bring the phone call I was hoping for.

Chapter 6

Kendall

I hadn't slept well at all the night before and this time it wasn't because of my nightmares. It was because every time I closed my eyes, I could see Tristan's face and my heart would start to race. I'd tossed and turned reliving the feeling of his hand touching mine. I lay there imagining how it would feel for his lips to be softly pressed against mine, to have his hands wrapped around my waist, to have them tangle in my hair as he deepened our kiss. It was something I'd always imagined but never dreamed could happen. Now, it was right in my grasp, but I'd backed off and I'd probably never hear from him again. My alarm had gone off, and I'd wanted to throw it across the room, but I managed to drag myself out of bed and into the shower. I tied my hair up into a bun and put on my work polo and a pair of Capris. I trudged down the stairs to the store and started a batch of cranberry muffins and some Danishes. I heard Becky call out that she was there and within a few moments the enticing aroma of coffee permeated the shop. I was drawn to it and made myself a cup. As I drank, I felt myself becoming human again and by the time George came in, I was my usual chipper self. He waved, grabbed the same book he'd been reading the day before and sat at his usual table. I poured his coffee and made my way over to greet him.

He peered up at me and said, "Kendall, you know I think the world of you but you look like hell. He carefully studied my face.

I plopped down in the chair across from him and sighed. "I didn't sleep well last night. I had a lot on my mind."

He took a sip of his coffee and smiled. "Good coffee, as usual." He paused then said, "Well, I don't know what's troubling you but I hope whatever it is, you get through it."

I patted his hand and returned the smile. "Thank you. I really appreciate that."

The doorbell chimed and I saw a group of young people come in so I jumped up to wait on them. A few minutes later, Averi popped in for her usual coffee and she gave me a strange smile before dashing back out. The morning went by quickly and I sold several books to some tourists. I was busy straightening up the bookshelves when I heard someone come in.

"Kendall? I think you'd better come here," George said.

Puzzled, I rounded the corner and saw a delivery man holding a huge bouquet of flowers in a gorgeous crystal vase. He looked down at his clipboard. "Are you Kendall Hart?"

Eyes wide, I nodded and walked over. "These are for you," he said holding out the clipboard for me to sign. "Hope you enjoy them!"

He handed the bouquet to me and with a smile was gone. I carried them over to the counter to set them down. Becky came out of the back and her mouth fell open. "Oh my gosh! They're beautiful!" George had even managed to pry himself away from his book to come investigate. They were beautiful Stargazer Lilies in the most vibrant pink I'd ever seen. They were breathtaking and their fragrance was incredible. With shaking hands, I pulled the card from the holder. I'd never gotten flowers from anyone before. I pulled the card out and when I saw who they were from I felt a little lightheaded. This just wasn't possible.

George looked over my shoulder and slid his reading glasses down on his nose. "Sounds like this Tristan likes you. You gonna call him?"

I looked back at him and laughed. "Honestly, I'd be a fool not to. They're my favorite flower."

Becky was grinning as she handed me my phone. "Go for it, Kendall. You deserve to have some fun. Let this guy take you out. If nothing else, it's a free meal," she said laughing.

I turned around to see George was headed back to his table and Becky quickly found something to keep busy. I dialed the number and held my breath.

"Tristan O'Neal…" I got chills instantly just from his voice.

"Um, hi. This is Kendall," I said softly.

"Kendall. I'm so glad you called." I loved the way he said my name and he sounded genuinely pleased to hear from me.

"I got my flowers. They're absolutely beautiful." I looked over at the bouquet and smiled.

I heard him cover the phone but could still hear him though it was muffled. "Tell Mr. Anderson I'll call him back in a few minutes." He uncovered the phone and said, "I'm sorry, I had another call but it's something that can wait."

I protested, "If you need to go…"

"Oh no, you're my number one priority right now. So, did my flowers convince you to take a chance on dinner with me?"

I could smell the sweet fragrance of the lilies drifting over to me. "They are very persuasive, I must admit. Tristan, I'm just not sure."

He was quiet for a moment then said, "I know something's holding you back but I promise you, I will be a perfect gentleman and if you don't ever want to see me again after our date, I'll back off and not bother you again."

My heart pounding I finally said, "Okay. I'll go."

"Well if you could see me now, I'm doing a victory fist pump right now. I stopped by the office to meet my new co-workers and now they're looking at me like I'm nuts but I really don't care. I've got two questions for you. First, when can I see your beautiful face again and second, do you mind riding a motorcycle?"

I blushed at his compliment. "Well, to answer your questions, I'm free any night this week and I'd love to ride with you. I've never been on a motorcycle before."

"Great! I'll pick you up tomorrow night. I need to get a few things before I take you riding. I'll pick you up at say, 7:30?"

"Sounds good, I'll be ready," I said looking over at George who was beaming.

"I can't wait, Kendall. See you tomorrow."

I heard the phone disconnect and felt Becky poke me in the side as she gave me a wink.

"So, you have a date! It's about time!" George said chuckling as he came over to pat me on the shoulder.

I started laughing. "I didn't realize my love life was so important to so many!"

Becky turned me to face her. "Kendall, you're a beautiful person, inside and out and it's about time you had some happiness. You're too young to be locked up in this store every day and night. I know you're doing it for your parents but they would want you to move on and have a happy life."

At the mention of my parents, I felt that familiar twinge of guilt that they weren't here and that my sister would never experience the things I was able to. I took a deep breath and nodded. "You guys are right. I need to find my happiness."

"Who got the pretty flowers?" Averi said walking through the front door.

I walked over to the bouquet and took a big sniff. "I did. They're from Tristan."

Her eyes grew wide. "THE Tristan?"

"Yes, you goofball…THE Tristan. He asked me to dinner."

"And?" She prompted, waving her hand at me impatiently.

"And, I'm going," I said grinning.

Averi pulled me in for a big hug. "Oh this is big…this is soooo big. Do you realize who asked you out? Hello? Only the man you've been fantasizing about for years! What are you going to wear? A mini skirt? Your cute denim shorts?"

"Um, probably not. He's picking me up on his motorcycle," I said walking to the kitchen. I glanced over my shoulder to see her mouth hanging open. I giggled and ran into the kitchen with her chasing behind me.

"His motorcycle? Kendall…you will be literally wrapped around him!" She leaned against the fridge. "I can't breathe. This is too freaking amazing."

I stopped giggling and grew serious. "Oh gosh, I will, won't I? Oh now I'm super nervous. Why did you have to tell me that?"

She shrugged. "I don't know, maybe because it's freaking amazing."

I had to laugh. Averi seemed more excited than I was. "I'm sure I'll just throw on some jeans and a cute shirt. I've never been on a motorcycle before," I said wiping down the kitchen. Averi stayed with me until closing and as I locked the door, I waved goodnight to her and went upstairs to my apartment. That night I slept like I hadn't slept in a long time and didn't have a single nightmare. I got up feeling refreshed yet with nervous anticipation. I dug through my closet and laid out my clothes in advance. I chose a plain white t-shirt, blue jeans, and a gray lightweight sweater. Averi had insisted I wear boots for safety and because as she put it, "They totally go together!"

I opened the store and greeted George who was already at the door. "Big night tonight, eh Kendall?" He asked with a wink. My stomach instantly knotted up. Throughout the day, Becky and George kept giving me a countdown to my date and even Averi got her two cents in via text messages. By the end of the day, I was sweating from every pore in my body and I just knew all the stress was going to cause me to break out.

Averi came over after she closed and checked out my outfit. "Very nice! Now, you know you just need to put your hair back in a ponytail or a braid because you're going to have helmet head regardless." I hadn't thought of that. I opted for the braid and put my makeup on. When I came out of the bathroom, she looked me up and down and gave me a thumbs up. "You look amazing. He won't know what hit him! I'm gonna get out of here but I want all the details!" She gave me a hug and dashed out.

At exactly 7:30, I heard the doorbell ring and felt my anxiety rise. With sweaty palms, I came down the stairs from my apartment and saw him standing at the door. He was dressed in a black t-shirt and jeans, his muscles being the first thing I noticed. He had his hair pulled back, and I could see his sparkling blue eyes watching me as I opened the door.

"Hi. You look amazing," he said taking my hand to his mouth where he brushed his lips across my skin. Again, I felt that spark of electricity. I found myself speechless at first but managed a smile then said, "Thank you…you do too." After locking the door, he walked me down the boardwalk keeping his hand on the small of my back. We rounded the corner leading to the parking lot, and I saw his bike for the first time. I felt excitement run through me but also a little fear. He walked me over to the bike and gestured to a helmet sitting on the seat. "I got that for you." He picked it up and slipped it over my head, his hands expertly tightening my chin strap then slid a pair of wrap sunglasses on me. He put on his own helmet and I noticed that mine matched his. "A few things we'll go over before we ride. I get on the bike first, then you climb on behind me. You have a back rest so you don't have to hold on tight," he paused, "unless you want to." He gave me a wink. "When we lean into a turn, just lean your body with me don't try to lean before we get there. You'll get the hang of it. And last, know that I'll do everything I can to keep you safe. Do you trust me?"

Nodding, I smiled. "Yes, I trust you," I said softly.

He climbed on the bike and got himself steadied then looked over his shoulder at me. "Just step on the foot board and climb on, just like you would mount a horse. I've got everything steady." Taking a deep breath, I put my hand on his shoulder, stepped on and swung my leg over to place it on the other foot board then sat down. I immediately was aware that my legs were straddling him, and my chest touched his back. Tentatively, I wrapped my hands around his waist and felt his abs flex under my touch. The heat of his body against mine was intoxicating, and it was then I noticed how good he smelled. The clean scent of soap from his skin drifted up, and I was in the middle of a big sniff when he turned his head to look at me. "You approve?" He teased, grinning.

I blushed furiously. "I do," I managed to stammer.

The bike started with a rumble, and I tightened my grip on his waist. He gave me a reassuring glance and pulled away from the parking lot and within minutes, we were cruising down the road. My senses were overloaded with sights, sounds and scents as we made our way down the beach highway. As the miles passed, I found myself relaxing and enjoying the wind on my face. As we entered every curve, I mimicked Tristan's body movements. I was in awe of the skill with which he handled the bike and the way his biceps flexed every time he accelerated the bike. I had to admit, it was super distracting. We made our way through traffic until we reached Wrightsville Beach where he turned into the parking lot for Oceanic. It was one of my favorite restaurants, and I was astonished to see this was our destination. He pulled the bike into a parking space and once we'd stopped, he told me it was okay for me to climb off. He secured the bike and helped unsnap my helmet. As I pulled it off, I cringed thinking how horrible my hair must look but the appreciative look in his eyes told me I looked just fine. He brushed a tendril of hair away from my cheek and then took my hand leading me to the restaurant. The hostess seated us on the pier giving a spectacular view of the Atlantic. The sun was low in the sky casting shadows on the beach and the few people doing their evening walks. The surf was fairly calm and the salty breeze was gentle. Our server came to take our drink orders and I noticed Tristan only ordered water. Seeing my puzzled look he responded, "I don't drink anything stronger than water when I'm on the bike. I've got precious cargo and I won't be taking any chances."

"Thank you. I've had dates where they started drinking before they even picked me up," I said laughing. "They always ended badly."

He furrowed his brows. "They must have been idiots. I'd want to remember every moment with you."

I could feel the color rush to my cheeks again. "Thank you. I'm honestly at a loss when you say things like that. I find it hard to accept compliments."

He leaned back in the chair and stroked his chin. "Kendall, you are hands down the most beautiful woman I've ever met and I have a hunch your beauty goes straight to your soul." My hands were trembling, and I tried not to let him see. Having him this close, him saying those things to me, it was almost more than I could bear.

The server arrived and as she placed our drinks on the table, she asked if we were ready to order. I hadn't even given the menu a thought and I panicked but Tristan, seeing my dilemma, spoke up. "I'd like to order for us. I think we'll start with the Hot Crab Dip appetizer and then for the main course we'll have the Lobster Fusilli with a side salad. Kendall, what kind of dressing do you prefer?"

I sat in stunned silence for a moment marveling at the choices he'd made and that they were all my favorites. "Um, Ranch dressing is fine," I said gazing at him in wonder.

Tristan turned to the server and said, "Make that two with Ranch. I love that dressing."

She wrote everything down then left us alone again. There was a measure of silence then he said, "So, how did you come to own a bookstore?"

I paused for a moment, thought carefully about my response then answered, "It was left to me."

Tristan's eyebrows raised slightly. "Really? That's a big responsibility. How long have you had it?"

I took a deep breath. "I inherited it almost five years ago. I was seventeen when I took over the store."

Shaking his head he said, "You must have been scared to death to take something like that on. Didn't you have any family to help you?"

To avoid explaining the reason I inherited it, I chose to steer the conversation away from it. "I have amazing grandparents who encouraged me to move to Simpsonville instead of taking over the store. They have a small farm where they raise cows and even have a donkey. I love them dearly but it wasn't what I wanted so I buckled down, took some night classes to finish high school then some college level classes in business. I've been doing pretty good with my little store."

He smiled. "I admire your drive and independence. Your store is more than just a place to buy books and have coffee. It seems to be a place to hang out with friends and that can only be because of you and your warm personality."

I laughed. "I guess so. I'm told I have a knack for making people feel comfortable…they say I don't know a stranger."

"I can believe it, there's something special in your eyes. I see compassion and patience but also something else I haven't put my finger on yet. I'm still figuring you out."

I felt my anxiety start to build as I expected the questions to come but instead he said, "I'd like you to meet my parents. They'd love you."

"Whoa there cowboy," I said laughing. "This is moving a bit fast for me."

He grinned. "I didn't mean right now. I meant eventually, if this goes past tonight. I'm keeping my fingers crossed."

I tilted my head to the side to study him. This was dangerous. My heart was screaming "OF COURSE IT WILL!" But my head was saying "You have so much baggage. He deserves someone who can be completely honest with him." I opened my mouth to respond just as the server brought our appetizer. We dipped our toasted buttered bread into the creamy crab dip, and I couldn't help but moan as I tasted it. Tristan gave me a wicked grin, and I found myself blushing once again.

We made small talk, leaving the really personal stuff off the table and I found out that he liked surfing and all sports and had been lucky enough to see the Panther's play while in Charlotte. I'd never been to a professional football game and listened as he described the excitement of being there. "I really like Dallas," I said cringing expecting the usual bashing that accompanied that statement.

He smiled broadly. "So do I!"

I laughed out loud. "Come on, you're just saying that."

He grew serious. "I'll have you know I've followed the Cowboys since I was five! Troy Aikman and Emmitt Smith were my favorite players!"

I laughed. "Who knew all these years later Emmitt would become a dance sensation!"

"And Troy Aikman would be giving the commentary!" He added joining in the laughter.

"So, surfing…I've always wanted to try that but I'm totally uncoordinated," I said laughing. "You're probably really good at it."

"Well, Ian and I've surfed since we could walk. My dad used to take us down to the beach to get us out of our mom's hair and we took to it like a duck does to water. I can't imagine you being uncoordinated about anything. Those gorgeous legs of yours are the perfect shape and your height would be a perfect balance, if you were taught properly. I'd love to show you sometime."

Blushing again, I nodded. "I'd like that."

From there on we talked about television and movies and found we had a lot in common. I'd always imagined him a certain way and he was totally smashing that image but in a good way making him even more attractive, if that were even possible. I found myself feeling more comfortable than I ever had on a date. It was truly the perfect evening.

"So, after dinner I thought we might take a ride down to Market St. They've got a Tutti Frutti down there and I think we'll be ready for some dessert by then."

"I would love it," I said. My heart was soaring at the thought of spending even more time with this beautiful man.

Chapter 7

Tristan

I felt myself falling hard. Kendall was intelligent, compassionate and sexy as hell, everything I'd dreamed of in a woman. A comfortable silence fell over us and I found myself becoming lost in her vibrant blue eyes. I couldn't help myself, I reached across to softly touch her face and felt her lean into my palm. "Being with you has been one of the best nights of my life," I said as I brushed my thumb softly across her silky skin. "I hope you feel the same way."

My heart leapt when she gave me a dazzling smile and nodded. "I do. I'll be honest, I've only had a handful of dates in my life and this is the best by far."

"So, have you ever been in a serious relationship?" I asked hoping she'd say no but knowing a beautiful woman like her had to have been.

"Only one. I met Ken when I was doing my night school classes. I won't say I was in love," she said before pausing as if in thought. "I guess our relationship was more like best friends who took it to another level really to just get it over with." She blushed then apologized for sharing too much with me. I was actually thankful that she did though. I wanted to know everything about her and any past relationships she'd had were an important part of who she was.

"I dated someone from high school," I confessed. "Her name was Maria. I thought she was what I wanted and like you, we carried it to the next level but when she got into a different college, she decided I wasn't enough. She cheated on me with some guy she went to school with. I confronted her then walked away." She listened in silence nodding when appropriate, but her smile faded when I said, "I saw Maria for the first time in years on the night I first saw you. She was prowling after me but I made it clear I wasn't interested." At that comment, a look of relief crossed her face, and her beautiful smile returned. "I'm really only interested in one person right now." I gave her a wink and was rewarded with another dazzling smile. We finished our dinner making comfortable small talk, and as we left the restaurant I took her hand. Once on the bike, she immediately put her tiny hands tightly around my waist, and I couldn't help but smile. This was heaven for me. I took the long way to Tutti Frutti and dessert in hand we walked down to the waterfront. The breeze was light, and we could see the lights of the battleship sparkling on the water. Kendall was quiet, seeming content just holding my hand tightly as we walked. We stopped in Riverfront Park and found a bench under a tree to sit on. The sun had almost set and the air was a bit chilly, so I wrapped my arm around her and pulled her close. She snuggled against my chest and I laid my cheek against her soft hair. "Tristan," she said softly. "Thank you for being so wonderful."

I lifted my head as she looked up at me. Her lips were within inches of mine and I was tempted to just kiss her but was afraid of moving too fast and scaring her off. I held her gaze and gradually felt her lean closer until her lips met mine. Sliding my hand up her arm, I could feel the softness of her sweater wishing it was her bare skin. Her lips tasted like peaches and were soft, warm, and moist. I ran my tongue lightly across her lips and felt her respond. As I deepened the kiss, I felt her hand slide around my waist to run up my shirt touching my bare skin. Cupping the nape of her neck while tangling my hand in her loose braid, I became aware we were in a public place so I pulled away but not before noticing the look of disappointment on her face. Catching my breath, I finally said, "I'm sorry, I hope I didn't come on too strong."

"Don't apologize," she said blushing, "you weren't the one who started it." She snuggled in close to me and we sat quietly watching the people strolling by. Eventually, I could feel her trembling from the breeze off of the water so despite it meaning the end of the evening, I reluctantly suggested I take her back home. Before we got on the bike, I unzipped my jacket and took it off. She looked at me with a puzzled expression. "What are you doing?" She asked.

"I'm making sure you're taken care of." Holding my jacket out to her, she balked but finally slipped her arms in and I zipped it up. "There you go. At least you won't be frozen by the time I get you back home."

"But Tristan," she protested. "You'll be cold. You're only wearing a t-shirt."

I laughed. "Kendall, I'm a big boy. Let me take care of you."

After a moment, she nodded. "Okay, but if you ever want to take me riding again, I'll be prepared."

I lifted her chin bringing her gaze to mine. "Not if, but when. I can't wait to take you out again. It's totally up to you."

She lowered her lashes demurely then looked back up at me with those blazing blue eyes. "I'd love that," she said softly.

I climbed on the bike and leaned toward her. I couldn't resist. I softly kissed her before she climbed on the bike.

We rode to her apartment and once there, I wrapped my arm around her waist as we walked to her door. I didn't want the night to end. She stopped in front of the door and turned to face me. "Tristan, I had so much fun tonight." I leaned my hand against the building and pressed my body in close. I brushed the stray tendrils of her hair away from her face. Her skin was so soft and creamy and I loved the light sprinkle of freckles across her nose and cheeks. We were nose to nose, breath to breath, and I slowly moved in closer to touch my lips to hers. She sighed against my mouth as I wrapped my arm around her tiny waist and pulled her tightly against me. We kissed until we were breathless and then suddenly, I heard my phone ring. Reluctantly, I pulled away to check and saw it was my mom.

"I'm so sorry, I need to take this. It's my mom," I said as I answered. "What's up, Mom?"

"Tristan, I hate to bother you but I can't find Ian anywhere. Your dad tried to get up and fell. He says he's not hurt and won't let me call an ambulance but I need help getting him back into bed." She sounded upset and frustrated.

"Mom, it's no bother. I'll be right there. I'm only about five minutes away."

"Thank you, sweetie. I'll turn on the outside light for you."

I hung up and sadly realized my night with Kendall was over. "Is your dad okay?" She asked with concern.

"Well, he fell and I need to help my mom get him up and into bed. Ian's missing as usual. Look, I'll call you tomorrow if that's okay. I want you to know I had an amazing time tonight and can't wait to see you again," I said wrapping my arms back around her waist.

She draped her arms around my neck and gave me a soft kiss. "Go. Take care of your dad. I'm off all day tomorrow. It's the only day, I'm closed."

Nodding, I reluctantly released her from my arms as she slipped my jacket off, handing it to me while giving me another quick kiss. I started jogging down the boardwalk and I glanced back to see her waving as I turned the corner. I dashed over to my parent's house and noticed still no Ian. As I walked in the door, my mom looked up with relief from where she was sitting on the floor beside my dad. "Thank you again, sweetie."

My dad looked up at me and his eyes were filled with pain. The look in his eyes also told me not to tell my mom. "So Dad, you trying to go jogging tonight?" I asked trying to make light of the situation.

With gritted teeth, he chuckled. "Sure am. I told your mother I was ready to run a marathon." I reached under his arms and lifted him as easily as a feather. I supported him as I led him to his bed and once I got him situated, I looked down at his thin frame and realized how quickly things were declining. I'd heard of cancer patients going down by the month but my dad was going down by the day. I sat on the edge of the bed resting my hand on his. "Katie, darlin'," he said looking at my mom, "could you bring Tristan and me some sweet tea?" Immediately, mom dashed off and as soon as she was out of sight, dad motioned for me to come close. Lifting his head from the pillow, he whispered, "Son, I'm feeling like crap and every day it's getting worse and worse. I just wanted to talk to you privately for a moment to make sure that you'll be there for your mom when my time comes."

I took a deep breath and nodded. "Dad, you know I will. You didn't even have to ask me," I replied softly.

"I know," he said laying his head back on the pillow. "I just had to hear it for my own peace of mind." A moment later, my mom came in carrying two glasses of tea. She put a flexible straw in the glass for my dad and he lifted his head to take a couple of long sips before laying back down with a sigh. "Thank you, sweetie."

She smiled and sat on the edge of the bed. I was about to take a big gulp of tea when my mom said, "So, how was it that you were so close by?"

I looked at her and shrugged my shoulders. "Well, I was out on a date. I was dropping her off when you called."

My mom's face fell. "Oh no. I didn't mean to interrupt your date."

"It's okay, Mom. I'll see her again." I reached over and patted her hand. "I'd also love to bring her by to meet you both."

She stood and came around to where I was sitting. She hugged my neck and gave me a kiss on the cheek. "We'd love to meet your friend…"

"Kendall," I finished for her.

"What a beautiful name. I'm sure she's really something special to catch your heart this quickly."

I nodded and smiled. "Yes, she's really special. I can't wait for you *both* to meet her," I said looking at dad.

My dad reached over and squeezed my hand. "I'm sure she's lovely. You bring her by soon." He was interrupted by the clatter of Ian walking through the door.

"I came as soon as I got your message," he said before glaring at me. "I guess I didn't need to rush. Looks like Tristan has everything under control."

Mom leapt to her feet. "Oh no, baby. I'm still glad you came. Your dad had a bad fall and it was just luck that Tristan was out on a date right around the corner."

I saw Ian's eyebrows raise and prepared for the inquisition. "Date? Bro, you've only been here two days and you got a date? Do I know her?"

Still wanting to keep this off of his radar, I threw him a bone but one that was out in left field. "Doubt it, she works in Wilmington. I met her when I stopped in at the office and we hit it off so I asked her out."

He looked at me curiously. "Hmm, well you certainly work fast. Must run in the family."

Shaking my head and rolling my eyes I said, "Ian, I'd rather not be compared to you, thank you very much."

I saw my mom give me 'the look'. "Boys, you'd better behave. I think your dad has had enough excitement for tonight. You can go, I've got it under control now."

Ian and I both hugged our dad and kissed our mom on the cheek. We walked out of the house and I saw Ian had driven his truck and perched in the cab were the two girls I'd seen at Averi's getting their henna done. When they saw me walking with Ian, they waved and giggled. Ignoring them, I walked over to my bike with Ian following behind me and he pulled me aside to whisper in my ear.

"So, would it be all right if I bring Natalie and Alicia back to our place? I'm willing to share," he said glancing back at the truck where the girls were still waving furiously.

"Ian, that would be a big NO! I'm letting you stay there but it's not turning into a frat house. You can go hang out with them wherever they're staying but I'm warning you, come home alone."

Ian scowled then turned and sauntered back to his truck. "Ladies, my brother is being an ass tonight and won't be joining us. Guess it's just us." He climbed in, slammed the truck door, and squealed out of my parent's driveway.

Shaking my head at his immaturity, I climbed on my bike and drove home. I did some more unpacking and hung a few pictures. A few hours later, I heard Ian's truck pull up into the driveway. Pulling back the curtains, I saw him climb out and gently shut his door. He was alone. When he walked in, I could see he was still upset about me laying down house rules, and he started to walk past me without a word, but I wasn't prepared to let him get away with that. I grabbed him by the arm and spun him around. "If you think you're going to use my house as a hotel for your hookups, you can go ahead and pack your crap right now." He looked at me with bloodshot eyes. "Were you drinking and driving?" I growled.

He took a deep breath and blew it out. "No. If you must know, I dropped off the girls then went down to the boardwalk. I sat on the beach and…" He took a hitching breath. "I lost it. What's happening to dad is more than I can handle." He rubbed his hand across his eyes.

I looked at Ian and instead of the selfish, arrogant brat I'd been cursing, I saw a scared, loving son who was scared to death of losing his dad. He turned to go to his room but I pulled him into a much needed hug. "We're in this together and we need to be strong for mom. She's going to need us more than ever…"

Chapter 8

Kendall

The sun streaming through my gently waving curtains woke me, and I stretched my arms over my head and pointed my toes. My mouth curved into a smile as I remembered the kisses that Tristan and I had shared. I heard my phone beep with a text message and lazily reached over to grab it and was surprised to see a message from him.

Grab your bathing suit and come downstairs!

I jumped from my bed and dashed to the window. Looking down, I couldn't see him because the awning was blocking my view but I heard my doorbell ring and knew he was definitely down there. I fired off a quick text.

Give me fifteen minutes

Flying around my room, I grabbed my bikini, hit the shower to shave and with my hair still damp, rushed downstairs. I hurriedly unlocked the door and practically ran into a surfboard that was perched next to the door.

"Good morning, beautiful," he said flashing his brilliant smile.

Eyebrows raised, I pointed at the board. "Are you serious?"

"Oh yes, my darlin'. Today's the day to see if you've got what it takes. I borrowed the board to see if you wanted to play in the surf with me today." He looked me up and down then waggled his eyebrows. "I'm also curious to see if that bathing suit will stay intact all day." I flushed with embarrassment.

"Oh gosh, I can't go in this, let me run back up to change." I started to run back inside but Tristan blocked the door with his arm.

"I've got a wetsuit you can wear. You don't need to change. Plus, I like the view." He waggled his eyebrows again and gave me a crooked smile.

This man was so irresistible and the way he looked at me made me feel so sexy. "Well, I'm glad you have the wetsuit because I don't think I want the tourists to run screaming from the beach," I said laughing.

He hefted the board with one arm like it was weightless and grasped my hand with the other. "The only thing running from the beach screaming will be any guys that look at you too long. They'll have to deal with me."

As we walked down the boardwalk, I realized how much I loved the feeling of my hand in his. When we reached the end of the boardwalk, we walked across the sand toward the water. The surf was choppy this morning because, as Tristan explained, there was a storm offshore. The waves were about four to six feet and we could see the avid surfers already paddling their way out to hopefully catch the 'big one'.

"Hey, Tristan!" We heard a voice calling down the beach and turned to see a man running down the beach carrying a surfboard.

"Pops! What's up? You hitting the surf?" Tristan asked as the man ran up to stand beside us planting his surfboard in the sand. As he nodded, Tristan introduced us. "Hoby, this is Kendall." Hoby was a really nice looking man, probably in his early forties sporting a stylish goatee and an amazing tan.

"Well, hello Kendall!" He said giving me a grin. "I know exactly who you are, I just don't drink coffee and try not to read. It strains my brain."

I had to laugh. "Well, at least you know about my place. I have some wicked muffins and scones too if you ever want to stop in and try them. I'll even rustle up a big glass of milk…you do drink milk? And, do I call you Pops or Hoby? Is Hoby short for anything?"

He gave me a wink. "I'd like you to call me Hoby. It's a nickname, short for Hobart. I let all the young wannabe surfers call me Pops. Gives me a little seniority on the waves. And to answer your milk question, sure do! I'll definitely have to stop by, especially now that I've seen how pretty you are. I totally understand why George stops by every day that you're open."

I laughed. "George is a fixture in my shop but I wouldn't have it any other way. I love him, he's a sweetheart." I saw Tristan's smile fading and I realized what that must've sounded like. I touched Tristan's arm and smiled. "George is an elderly man who loves my coffee and my books. He's been coming in regularly ever since his wife passed away a few years ago."

Tristan's smile grew bright again as he wiped his forehead. "Whew. I thought I was gonna have some competition. I'll need to meet him, he sounds irresistible." He gave me a wink that made my heart beat faster.

Hoby grinned and moved to put his arm around my shoulder. "Dude," he said giving me a squeeze. "There's always gonna be competition when a lady looks this gorgeous. I'm a sucker for a redhead!" He gave me a flirty wink. "You're just lucky I'm a happily married man." He grabbed his board and with a devilish grin splashed into the surf to begin paddling out past the breakers. I watched in awe as he lay on his board watching the waves rising behind him then as the wave started to crest, he started paddling furiously toward shore. Just as the wave started to break, he rose effortlessly and balancing perfectly, rode the wave toward shore. I felt a nervous knot form in my stomach thinking of how absolutely ridiculous this whole idea was. My palms were sweating as I looked over to find Tristan studying my face.

"You okay? You look a little green." He walked over and softly touched the side of my face. "Are you nervous? I promise, I won't ever let you get hurt."

Just the touch of his hand helped to calm my nerves and I gave him a smile. "I just don't want to look like a dork," I finally admitted.

He stepped closer and lifted my chin forcing my eyes to meet his. "Kendall, you could never look like a dork in my eyes. You're beautiful." He softly kissed my lips lingering for a moment then gently kissed my forehead. "You're going to do great. Let's get you on the board." I slipped on the wetsuit and was very conscious of how body-hugging it was. After another appreciative look from Tristan, he had me limber up then watch more of the surfers and their techniques. Finally, when he was satisfied I'd gotten the gist of things, we splashed into the water mimicking Hoby's style and he lay the board on the surface of the water. "I'll hold the board while you just get the feel of the ocean. Let your body move with the motion of the waves. I'll be right here beside you."

I did as instructed while tightly holding on but allowing my feet to dangle in the water. Small waves were rolling in and the first few came over the front of the board swamping it but pretty soon I was balancing enough to keep the front up out of the water. Tristan stood patiently beside me giving me pointers but also watching the surf to make sure that I didn't get surprised by a rogue wave. He then slipped the leash from the board around my ankle and pushed me out into deeper water. I saw Hoby straddling his board, watching with curiosity, which made me nervous. "Let's try to get you riding a wave on the board first," Tristan said laying his hand on the small of my back. He turned me toward the shore and as a small wave came, he pushed me forward and magically, the board caught the wave. I could feel the power of the ocean, although on a small scale, and it felt amazing to glide with the wave into shore. The board ground to a halt on the sand and I stood to pick up the board and found Tristan right beside me. "So? How did you like that?" He asked smiling broadly.

"Well, I have to admit that was fun! I just can't imagine doing that standing up, though. I can barely stand up on dry land," I said laughing.

Tristan wasn't laughing with me. "I just don't know how you can lack self-confidence. You're so much better than you think you are…in every way," he said wrapping me in his arms and pulling me against him. He lowered his head and when our mouths met, I felt that familiar spark run all over my body. "Mmm," he said as he pulled away slightly. "Your lips drive me wild." Breathless, I could only gaze into his ice blue eyes that were sparkling from the reflections off the water.

The moment was interrupted by the sound of Hoby shouting. "Hey you two! You're missing some awesome waves!"

Tristan waved his hand in Hoby's direction but kept his eyes locked on mine. "Kendall, I know this is crazy but I'm already having feelings for you and I'm afraid I'll scare you away. Do you think it's possible to fall in love with someone at first sight?"

I held my breath and swallowed hard before answering. "I do," I answered softly. The memory of falling into his arms all those years ago was still as fresh as the day it had happened and now I was wrapped in those same arms hearing him say he may be falling in love with me. It had to be a dream. He kissed my forehead and pulled me close to him. I laid my cheek against his bare rockhard chest and could hear the rapid thud of his heart. We stood like that for a few moments then he gently pulled me away to kiss me once again.

Clearing his throat, he murmured, "We'd better get back to your surf lesson before I throw you over my shoulder and take you somewhere private."

I stepped closer and wrapping my arms around his waist, nuzzled his neck. "I wouldn't mind going somewhere private," I whispered.

He groaned and pulled me tighter in his arms. "You're killing me, you know that, right?"

I smiled against his skin and could taste the salt on my lips. "I wouldn't want that to happen. We'd better get back to the surf lesson." I could feel his reluctance to release me, but finally, he relaxed his hold on me and reached over to grab the surfboard.

"Okay, let's see if you can stand on the board. If you feel like you're going to fall, just throw yourself away from the board so it doesn't hit you." I turned to head toward the water and felt the tug of the leash on my ankle. "Where do you think you're going?" He asked laughing.

"I'm going to stand on the board," I said indignantly putting my hands on my hips. I watched as he lay the board on the sand out of the reach of the surf.

"You're going to practice on the shore, first." He pulled me over by the leash to stand behind the board. He dug out divots to set the fins in and then gave me my stand up lesson. I was really trying to pay attention but when he put his hands on my hips to center them on the board, I lost all track of what I was doing. He calmly explained how to place my hands and how to pop up to a standing position. I finally found my focus as I realized this might actually be dangerous if I didn't pay attention. When he was satisfied with my technique, he moved the board out into the water with me trailing behind. He'd shown me how to paddle out so as I did so, he swam beside me. We got past the breakers and met up with Hoby who'd just come back out from riding a really nice wave. Tristan used Hoby's board to hang on to while I got situated facing the shore. I heard him talking to Hoby but couldn't make out what they were saying. The waves were gently passing and I let myself softly roll over them. I felt Tristan swim beside me and as I looked over, he was looking behind me. "Okay, Kendall. Get ready and just relax and enjoy the ride." I looked behind me and saw a nice wave rolling lazily toward me and knew this was the one. "Don't forget to paddle a couple of times as the wave picks you up," he said checking my board position one last time. My heart was hammering in my chest, and my mouth felt like cotton, but I took a deep breath and as the wave lifted me, I paddled two times and planted myself just like he'd shown me. I popped up to find myself actually standing on my feet and using my arms for balance, I kept myself upright and pointed toward shore. The feeling of surfing was incredible and I instantly regretted not having done this sooner. I focused on watching where I was going but soon realized the shore was fast approaching, and I panicked. Losing focus, I started pinwheeling my arms making me lose my balance and within seconds, I felt myself falling off the board. The salty swirling water surrounded me and instinctively, I took a breath. Quickly, I discovered that was the wrong thing to do as the water filled my lungs. I fought to find the surface and felt the board pulling me toward the shore where I bumped along the bottom. Suddenly, I felt strong arms wrapping around me pulling me free of the surf. Coughing and spluttering, I surfaced to see Tristan's worried face. "Oh my God, Kendall. Are you okay?" I couldn't speak, only wheeze and cough. I could feel the salt water burning my lungs. Tristan quickly unsnapped the leash from my ankle and carried me to the beach where he lay me down on the sand. I couldn't catch my breath and my eyes were watering from where I'd opened them when I had my panic attack.

"You scared me, baby!" His eyes were so full of concern.

I coughed a few more times and finally was able to breathe. "I think I'm okay. I swallowed water." I coughed a few more times as I turned on my side and Tristan rubbed my back.

Hoby ran up to us and knelt beside me. "Wow, kid. I've never seen anything like that."

I managed a weak smile. "You've never seen a graceful dismount like that before?"

He shook his head no. "I've never seen a first timer ride like that. You were a natural…until you lost your focus. I'm really impressed!"

I lay on the sand taking slow, even breaths until I felt my heart return to a normal pace. I rolled over onto my back and slowly sat up. It was then I realized Hoby was part of a crowd around me full of tourists of all shapes and sizes. One small boy stood staring at me, shovel and pail in hand. "Mommy, is the lady gonna be okay?" He asked, never taking his eyes off of my face.

"Sure, honey," his mother said while trying to hold his hand and balance a little girl on her hip. "She just swallowed some water…her boyfriend is making sure she's okay."

I heard the boyfriend part and started to protest to save Tristan embarrassment but before I could, he said, "That's right. I'm going to take good care of her." He scooped me effortlessly into his arms and carried me back to my apartment. Once there, he insisted on unlocking the door and carrying me up the stairs despite my protests. Once in my apartment, I insisted I was steady enough to take a shower. He informed me that he'd be waiting outside and for me to call if I needed him. When I got in the bathroom, I looked in the mirror and realized I looked absolutely hideous. I could see tiny shells stuck to the side of my face and sand caked in my hair along with a couple of abrasions on my elbows and knees from scraping the shells as I tumbled to the shore. I climbed into the shower and lathered up my hair and scrubbed myself clean. The warm water soothed me and in no time, I was feeling like myself again. Climbing from the shower, I wrapped a big fluffy towel around myself and took a small towel to take most of the water out of my hair. I grabbed a comb and dragged it through my now damp hair then slipped on my robe that I had hanging on the back of my bathroom door. As I opened the door, my heart stopped. Tristan was holding the picture of my family in his hand and as he turned to face me, I could see I was going to have to explain, at least the part I could.

"That's my family," I said my voice breaking. "They died in a fire."

Tristan looked back at the picture and with his fingers, gently touched the glass as if making contact with those who'd meant the world to me. "Kendall, you don't have to talk about it. I can see it's upsetting you and I can't imagine how horrible that must have been."

Taking a deep breath I walked over to stand beside him, my eyes focused on the picture. "It happened almost five years ago. I wasn't home when the fire started and by the time I got there, the house was engulfed. They found everyone still in their beds. The fire investigator said they probably died of smoke inhalation before the fire got to them. I pray that's true…" I felt the tears threatening and fought them by taking a deep cleansing breath. "I try not to talk about it because it's still just as painful as if it happened yesterday." Without a word, he reached over and took my hand then slowly turned my wrist over. I looked down at the intricate tattoo watching as he gently rubbed his thumb over the initials etched in my skin.

"You did this for them," he said as if he knew the whole story. I felt a tear run down my cheek as I nodded. "Is this their initials?"

"Yes," I said softly. "My dad was Charles, my mom was Helen…and my sister was Kelsey." I said my voice breaking. "I got this one too, just for Kelsey." I slid the sleeve of my robe up to show him the flower on the inside of my upper arm. He leaned closer as if to see it better but instead placed a tender kiss on my skin.

"You've been through so much, yet you have to be one of the strongest people I've ever known." Still holding my wrist, he pulled me into his arms. I tucked myself against his chest and felt his arms wrap around me. He nuzzled my cheek, and I could feel his breath against my skin. It was so quiet I could hear his heart beating rapidly in his chest. He kissed my cheek then brushed his nose against my neck murmuring, "God, you smell so good. Me, not so much." I tried to laugh but the shivers up and down my spine as his lips moved up my neck to the lobe of my ear where he nipped playfully were totally distracting me.

"Well, you're welcome to take a shower, if you'd like to freshen up," I murmured. I slid my hands down his bare chest feeling the ripples of his abs under my fingers, and I heard his breaths becoming more rapid to match my own. He pulled away to cup my face with his broad hands, his eyes blazing with desire. "I'll be two minutes."

He dashed into the bathroom, and I heard the shower come on. Immediately, I dashed into my closet and dragged out my single girl's survival kit that Averi had given me for my twenty-first birthday. It had been meant as a humorous incentive to get a man but ended up on the top shelf taking up space. I opened the box and found Averi had thought of everything. I silently thanked her for being such a goof but also saving us a trip to the local pharmacy.

I grabbed some supplies and threw them into the nightstand. I was probably jumping the gun, but I was also being prepared. I grabbed a comb and pulled the tangles out of my damp hair. I heard the shower shut off so I grabbed some lotion and lathered it on finishing up just as the door to the bathroom opened. I had to struggle to keep my mouth from falling open at the sight of Tristan standing there only in a towel. He had it slung low on his hips showing off his well-defined V. His hair was wet and hung down to his shoulders. He walked over wearing a sexy smile and wrapped me in his arms. "Did you miss me?" He growled in my ear. I nodded then pulled back to brush my lips lightly against his. He slanted his mouth capturing mine in a heated kiss. As his warm lips caressed mine, I ran my hands up his chest to his hair which I tugged to deepen the kiss. I released his hair by gently running my fingers through its silky softness, and I heard him growl from deep in his chest. His hands found the front of my robe and he gently tugged the belt loose allowing the robe to fall open. His eyes hungrily devoured me as he slid his hands inside the robe to caress my still damp, bare skin. I shrugged the robe off of my shoulders and let it fall to the floor never taking my eyes off of his. "Oh, baby," he said before capturing my mouth with his once again but this time with an urgency, a desire that we couldn't deny any longer. He backed me toward the bed as I released his towel which fell to the floor. I had to take a moment and admire the perfect body in front of me. We kissed again. Our naked bodies now pressed together as we fell onto the bed. Tristan rolled me onto my back still kissing me, and I felt dizzy, almost drunk with desire. He trailed his lips from my eager mouth down my neck to the hollow of my throat where I could feel his tongue lapping my skin between his kisses. His hands were strong but gentle as they explored my body. Closing my eyes, I found myself arching into him, aching for more. The electricity in the air was palpable, as if there was a wicked thunderstorm approaching. My hands clasped his broad shoulders, and I found myself tangling my fingers in his hair urging him not to stop. My heart was thundering in my chest, and I saw him lay his head on my chest for a moment, and a smile played on his lips. He looked up at me, and I saw a serious expression come across his face. "Kendall, I'm…I didn't come prepared for this."

It took me a moment to understand what he was saying since my mind was still spinning from the sensations of his body so close to mine. "Oh," I said pointing to the bedside table drawer, "I got a single girls survival kit for my birthday one year but I've never opened it."

He gave me blinding smile. "Don't move," he said before leaving me for a moment. I lay there blushing, touching my finger to my lips where his had been just a few moments before. I actually pinched myself to make sure this wasn't a dream. My eyes were drawn to him and immediately, I felt the flush of desire coursing through my body.

He returned to the bed and captured my mouth with his and kissed me until I was breathless. His strong hands drifted across my skin sending sparks throughout my body. I heard a sharp intake of his breath and saw he was looking at the abrasions on my skin. He tenderly kissed each one as he said, "I'm so sorry, baby," his voice muffled against my skin. "I won't ever let you get hurt again." I was so touched by the raw emotion in his voice and it only fueled my desire. I tentatively reached out and touched him and with a hiss, his eyes fluttered shut. Having dreamt of this for years, I discovered my dreams had been nothing compared to reality. Every muscle on his perfect body was taut and defined and as my hands passed over him, his chest began to heave with every breath. Suddenly, he grasped my hand, kissed my tattoo on my wrist and lay me back against the pile of pillows. Moments later, his body was covering mine. Wrapping my calf around his leg, he palmed my thigh, kneading it with his fingers. Our kisses were feverish, we were insatiable. Any fears I had about being awkward or self-conscious were erased by the look in his eyes. When the time was right, our bodies melted into each other as our eyes met and all of the emotions I'd been holding back came pouring out of me. I surrendered myself to him completely and he took me with such tenderness and affection that I felt as if my heart would explode with love. We made love until we both came crashing back to reality, our heartbeat's slowing, our ragged breaths eventually returning to normal.

Chapter 9

Tristan

Kendall was amazing. I lay watching her sleep, her eyelashes fluttering slightly, her breathing soft and steady. I couldn't get enough of her. I lay my arm across her and unconsciously, she wrapped her hand around my arm tucking herself closer to me. I didn't want to leave her, but I knew I had to. It was late, and I needed to check in with my parents. I softly kissed her pouty lips and she stirred, until finally her eyelids fluttered open.

"Oh, gosh. Did I fall asleep? I'm so sorry!"

"Don't worry about it, baby. We both needed a nap," I said with a wink.

Her face flushed and she gave me a shy smile. "But it was a good tired...no bad dreams," she said giving me a gentle kiss.

I found myself wanting her again but saw by the clock that it was almost midnight. "I agree and on that note, it's late. I need to run by and check on the folks and we both have to work tomorrow."

I could see disappointment cloud her face but she shook it off with a smile. "Oh yeah, back to work. So, you start your new job tomorrow? How exciting."

Brushing back the strand of hair across her forehead, I kissed her softly. "Not as exciting as being with you." I trailed my fingers along her jaw pulling her gently toward me. I rested my forehead on hers so we were eye to eye. "I don't want to leave," I said softly.

"I don't want you to leave, but I understand," she whispered. "We can get together again soon, I hope."

I smiled. "You can count on it. I'll call you tomorrow night and see how your day was." She nodded as I climbed from the bed, the thought of leaving her gnawing at me. I got dressed and gave her a final kiss goodnight. "Sweet dreams, baby," I said as I left shutting the door behind me.

As I was leaving the shop and locking the door behind me, I heard a noise. I turned to see a guy leaning against the railing on the boardwalk. He was dressed in all black, and as I came out, he turned to give me a quick glance then turned back to look out over the moonlit beach. I called my mom knowing she'd still be up giving dad the last meds of the day and sure enough, she answered on the first ring.

"Hello?"

"Hey Mom, it's me. Just checking in on dad and to see if you need anything."

"We're okay, honey. How are you? Did you enjoy your day?" She asked before whispering to my dad, "It's Tristan."

"Sure, I had a great day. How's dad feeling?"

She hesitated. That scared me. "He had a bad day but he's resting comfortably now. He really hasn't eaten much today which makes me worry, but he says he's just not hungry."

"Do you need me to come by? I'm nearby," I asked getting on my bike.

"No, honey. Just go home and get some sleep for your big day tomorrow."

Leave it to my mom to make sure I was taken care of. "Well, I'll check in on the way home tomorrow, okay? Did you see Ian today?"

I heard her take a deep breath, "No. He called and said he had a life-guarding job today so I didn't expect him."

I shook my head. He had been lying in bed when I left this morning and when I asked what he was going to be doing, he mumbled something about having a day off and not having to do anything. I seriously doubted he'd gotten a call after I left since most of the guards were contacted the night before to make sure they were on the beach early.

"Well, you and dad call me if you need anything…night or day." I told her goodnight then slipped on the jeans and jacket I'd brought to change into for the chilly ride home. I was just about to crank my bike when I heard the guy I'd seen earlier yell to get my attention.

"Hey, you live around here?" He asked as he jogged up to me.

"Not far, why? What do you need?" I watched him closely for signs he wanted to "borrow" my money or worse, my bike.

"Uh, I was just wondering. I'm not from around here and I was supposed to meet a buddy of mine on the boardwalk but he never showed up. I know he lives near where the party boats go out so we planned to meet here."

I chuckled. "Dude, you're at the wrong beach. You're probably talking about Carolina Beach and that's a few miles up the road toward Wilmington. You may want to call him and tell him you're lost."

He rolled his eyes and shuffled his feet. "Well I would but my phone died," he said sheepishly. "You mind if I call him from yours?"

I pulled my phone from my pocket and handed it to him. "Do you know his number? Most people have them stored in their phone and can't remember them."

He nodded and started dialing. "Yeah, I can remember it like it's my own." I could hear his call connect but go to voicemail. "Hey, it's me. I'm at the wrong damn beach. My phone died so I'll head that way and hope you're still waiting for me."

He ended the call and handed the phone back to me. "Thanks…"

"Tristan," I finished for him.

"Tristan, nice to meet you. I'm Sebastian." We shook hands, and I wished him good luck finding his friend.

I pulled up in front of the house and saw Ian's bike was gone. Unlocking the door, I threw my keys on the table in the foyer, switched on the lights and turned on the tv. I grabbed a cold drink and threw myself on the couch. A few minutes later, I heard Ian drive up and come clattering up the steps.

"Hey, bro," he said throwing his keys down next to mine. "You just get home?"

I sat up and motioned for him to sit in the chair next to me. "We need to talk."

He looked at me uneasy but walked over and sat down. "What's on your mind?"

I looked at him and realized it was time to cut the crap and talk serious. "So, tell me…when are you gonna get your shit together? It's time to grow up."

He looked startled for a moment then I saw his shoulders slump. "You want the truth?"

I laughed. "Yeah man, I've always wanted the truth."

He took a deep breath. "Well, the truth is that I'm in love with someone who'll never want me so I really don't give a crap about my life or being anything better than I am."

I shook my head in disbelief. "How can you say that? Has she told you she doesn't want to be with you?"

He nodded. "Yes, actually she has."

"Do I know her?" I asked curiously. I had a feeling I knew the answer to this but wanted to be sure. He looked away as if deciding whether he could confide in me. "Ian, I'm not going to tell anyone."

Finally, he looked at me. "Funny enough, you met her the other day. You were in her henna shop."

I tried to act surprised. "Averi something?"

He bowed up a little. "Her name is Averi Rain. I've had my eye on her for a long time but she won't give me the time of day."

I lay my head back on the couch and closed my eyes. "Ian, what do you expect? You're constantly running around with two or three girls at a time! How can she respect you or think anything other than you're a player?"

He was silent, so I opened my eyes to look at him and saw him hanging his head down. "She's an amazing person and I just don't feel good enough for her. I know she looks down on me, she always has. I hang around outside the coffee shop next door hoping to see her going in or out but usually one of my ex's shows up as she's walking by and she gives me a drop dead look."

Seeing his depressed look, I really felt sorry for him. "Tell you what. I'll help you reform your image but it's going to take time and you're going to have to stay away from the Beach Bunnies," I said slapping him on the shoulder. "And I'm glad you told me what was bothering you. You've been on the wrong path and now we're going to set you straight."

"Tristan, do you think you could help me get a better job? One that's not beach related?" He asked pleadingly.

"Well, I'll be honest with you, you're not going to impress anyone with a resume consisting of lifeguard and surfing coach. I tell you what...I start my new job tomorrow and I'll see if there are any entry level jobs available. But I will tell you this, if I can find something open, I'll call you and you'd better be on your way over. You'll need to show them you're hungry and have initiative."

He nodded. "Okay, I'll get up when you leave so I can be ready, just in case." We talked a little about what skills he had, and I found that he'd taken some courses at Brunswick Community College but couldn't find his niche, so he hadn't gone back. I never knew about any of this and told him so. "Well, anything I did would never measure up to you so I told mom not to tell you."

"Ian, when are you going to learn that I'm not perfect. I have flaws. I failed statistics and had to take it over again in the summer. That was the year I didn't come home for summer break. I told mom and dad that I'd gotten a good job but I was actually working at a pizza place in Asheville. The owner, Mrs. Palmisano, was so nice to me and encouraged me to do better. She said, "If you want to be in business, you've got to be ALL business," I said imitating her heavy Italian accent.

We both ended up laughing but Ian suddenly became serious and said, "Well, I want to do better...For a lot of reasons."

"It's never too late to change," I said stretching. "And speaking of late, it's time to hit the bed. I've got to get up early…and so do you!"

We both said goodnight, and I headed to my room. I picked up my phone and saw a message from Kendall from only a few minutes before.

Thinking of you. Sweet dreams.

Hoping it wasn't too late, I texted back.

My sweet dreams will be of you. Goodnight, baby.

I saw her typing back right away.

Miss you already.

I smiled picturing her lying in her bed, hair fanning the pillow.

I'll see you again soon. Promise.

I waited for a response but after a few minutes realized she'd probably gone to bed. I crawled under the covers and lay on my back with my hands cradling my head wishing she were laying with me wrapped in my arms. I finally turned on my tv in the bedroom, set the sleep timer and within moments was fast asleep.

The shriek of my alarm woke me, and I tapped the snooze button hoping for just five more minutes. When the alarm went off again, I turned it completely off and dragged myself out of bed. After a quick shower, I got dressed in my new suit, brushed my hair back tying it up neatly, and slipped into my new dress shoes. As I walked by Ian's room, I heard him moving around so I made some coffee and when it was ready, knocked on his door. "Hey, I've got some fresh coffee out here if you're interested."

He opened the door and grinned. "If you need me today, I'll get a ride up there."

I waved goodbye, jumped in the truck and headed into Wilmington. The bank I was working in was in the heart of downtown, but I made good time driving in and was soon in the HR office filling out necessary paperwork and getting my employee handbook. It was the perfect opportunity to ask about any openings. The HR director told me that they actually did have an opening for an entry level employee and that they were going to start interviewing the next day.

I called Ian and told him to come by the bank and fill out an application, and he actually showed up. I saw him give me a thumbs up as he went into the HR office and then I got caught up in the craziness of the day and never saw him leave. At five o'clock, I was ready to head home and shake off the day. I called Kendall on the way home and she had had a busy day as well. "How about dinner?" I asked hopefully.

She didn't hesitate. "Sounds great! Just come over whenever you get ready. I'll be waiting."

"Okay, I'll see you in a little bit." I hung up and saw I'd missed a call. It was an unknown number, and they didn't leave a voicemail, so I chalked it up to a wrong number.

An hour later, I pulled my bike up in the parking lot by the boardwalk and jogged to her door. She was sitting in the cafe by the door and her face lit up when she saw me. I noticed she was wearing a light jacket and had to smile. "I told you I'd be prepared," she said giving me a kiss.

"Mmm, a perfect way to end the day," I said sweeping her into a hug as I nuzzled her neck. I heard her give a little squeal and a giggle. "Is someone ticklish?"

She gave me the most serious face she could without bursting out laughing. "No, I am NOT ticklish. I swear."

"Me thinks you are lying, beautiful lady." I nuzzled her neck again and heard the giggle again. "Hmm, I think I'll have to save this information for later," I said giving her an exaggerated wink.

Her eyes grew wide as she still fought the giggles. "Don't even think about it!"

"Well, we'll just have to see when I have my way with you."

She gave me an astonished look and in her best Southern belle accent, she said, "Why Mr. O'Neal. I do believe you're assuming you can have your way with me later."

Taking her cue, I bowed. "I'm so sorry if I offended Miss Kendall, I meant to ask properly if I could court you later," I drawled.

She batted her eyelashes. "Well, that's more like it. That would be most pleasurable." She purred out the last part making me want to skip dinner all together but I knew she'd had a busy day and needed nourishment.

"Woman, you are insatiable," I said laughing.

She looked up into my eyes and without hesitation said, "Only for you."

I wrapped my arm around her and proudly walked her to my bike. I took note of the appreciative glances she got from a majority of the guys on the boardwalk and pulled her just a little closer. We rode to a local seafood restaurant and while we waited for our dinner, we compared our days. She told me George had come in, as usual, and had actually bought a book. It was a new novel by Nicholas Sparks, his favorite author. Kendall told me his reason for buying it was that he was going to be traveling to New Bern soon for a book signing. He wanted to be prepared with his copy before he got in line. I could tell when she talked about him that he meant a lot to her, and I made a mental note to stop by there one morning and meet this George. We ate our dinner until we were stuffed and groaning, we climbed back on the bike. "Hey baby, I need to pick something up that I need for work, do you mind going with me?"

Kendall leaned around giving me a smile. "Is it a new suit or tie? I love ties." She gave me a naughty wink, and I shook my head as I chuckled.

I cranked the bike and headed toward Wilmington. As I turned in the car dealership, Kendall looked around with surprise.

"Are you buying a car?" She squealed with excitement.

I nodded as I parked the bike. "Yeah, I need a real car to drive to work in. My suits aren't very bike friendly."

A salesman came bounding out as we started looking over the cars on the lot. "Good evening," he said, his eyes lingering on Kendall just a little too long for my taste.

"Ahem," I said to get him to look at me. "I've already done some shopping online and I know you've got a couple I'm interested in." He finally shifted his eyes over to me and when he saw the expression on my face, he quickly began sucking up to me.

"Yes, sir. Do you have the models?" I handed him a piece of paper and he dashed off to find them on the lot.

"So," Kendall said tucking her hand in the crook of my arm. "If you've already picked them, what am I here for?"

I looked at her and smiled. "Well, I want your approval. I've done all the preliminary stuff, I just want to know which one you like best."

After about ten minutes, the winded salesman came back with a smile. "I got a couple of the other guys to pull them around so you can check them out side by side." He led us to the side of the building where there were two vehicles gleaming under the lights. There was a charcoal gray F-150 and a black 4 door Jeep Wrangler. I looked at Kendall's face and she was seriously studying both and then looking back at me as if picturing me in either one.

"So, baby? Which one?" I said pushing her gently toward them. She walked over, opened the door and started checking out the interiors of both then turned to me with a smile.

"I think the one that suits you best is the Jeep. It's practical for the bank days but you can take the top down and the doors off on beach days. I do believe your surfboard will fit in here too!"

I grabbed her into a big hug and swung her around. "A woman who thinks of everything! I'm not letting you out of my sight!"

She giggled and breathlessly said, "I hope not."

I glanced at the salesman who was now giving me an envious look and said, "I'm getting the Jeep." He hopped into action and within an hour we had finalized the paperwork and it was all mine. "Looks like you get to drive her home for me," I said passing the keys to Kendall.

She squealed and jumped in the driver's seat. "I'll follow you to your house and then you can take me home," she said cranking the Jeep.

We rolled through the streets of town eventually pulling up in front of my house. I was relieved to see Ian wasn't home because I still wasn't ready for him to meet her yet. I had her park in the driveway and after she'd climbed out, she smiled and said, "I love your new Jeep!

It's amazing to drive!" She looked around at the house. "So this is your place. Nice!"

"You want to come up and see it?" I said heading to the stairs. At that moment my phone rang. I saw unknown caller pop up and curiously, I answered. "Hello?"

I listened for a moment and heard only silence before I heard the beep indicating the call had ended. "Guess they didn't want to talk to me," I said laughing. A moment later, the phone rang again and this time MOM showed up. As I answered, I could tell she was upset.

"Tristan," she said sounding as if she were holding back tears. "I think we're going to need to take your dad to the hospital. He's not doing well and he doesn't want to be here at home. I feel he'd be more comfortable here but he's insisting I call for an ambulance."

I closed my eyes and took a deep breath. "I'll be right there. Don't do anything yet." I hung up and saw Kendall's concern. "It's my dad. He wants to go to the hospital and I think it's to spare my mom the pain of him passing at home."

I saw tears well in her eyes. "Oh Tristan, I'm so sorry. Listen, you go and I'll find a way home. I can call Averi to come pick me up." She gently placed her hand on my cheek. "I wish there was something I could do to help."

I pulled her into my chest and kissed the top of her head. "Come with me," I said wiping the tear that spilled onto her cheek.

Hugging me tightly, she nodded looking into my eyes. "Okay," she whispered.

We were driving to my parent's house when I got another call from my mom. "Tristan? We're on our way to the hospital. We couldn't wait."

I made a u-turn and headed toward New Hanover Regional. Kendall reached over and slipped her hand in mine. I glanced over as I gave it a gentle squeeze. "Thank you."

"I wouldn't be anywhere else," she said returning the squeeze.

When we arrived at the medical center, we checked in at the Emergency Department and were told my dad had been taken back to be evaluated and would be moved to a room within an hour or so. The nurse informed me that my mom was waiting in the lobby, so we headed through the crowd of people waiting to be seen and found her seated by a window clutching a cup of coffee. Kendall stopped walking and when I looked at her, she had a look of surprise on her face. "That's your mom?" She said looking at my mom with disbelief. Before I could answer, she stepped behind me and whispered, "Maybe I shouldn't be here. This is private family time."

"Why?" I said confused.

"Kendall?" My mom was rising from the chair with a look of recognition on her face. She turned to me with eyebrows raised. "Tristan, is this your special someone?"

Sheepishly, I nodded. "Apparently, you two know each other."

They both nodded and gave each other a tight hug. Seeing my confusion, my mom explained, "I've known Kendall for quite a while. I love her sweet little store."

Kendall turned to my mom. "I had no idea you were Tristan's mom! I wondered why you hadn't been by. I had no idea what you've been going through."

"It's been rough," my mom admitted. "I'm just so thankful that I have Tristan and Ian to help me."

"You talking about me behind my back again?" I heard Ian say as he came around the corner. He stopped in his tracks and stared at Kendall. "Red! What are you doing here?"

Kendall chewed her lip nervously, and I could tell by her reaction, she apparently knew Ian as well. I stepped into his line of sight. "She's here with me."

He had an incredulous expression on his face. "This is who you've been seeing?"

I stepped closer to him, "Yeah, so what."

He took a step back. "Hey, it's all good. I just had no idea this was your mysterious lady." An amused smile seemed stuck on his face as he dropped into one of the waiting room chairs. "Kendall Hart," he muttered. "Who would have guessed?"

"Umm, I think I'll grab some coffee for everyone," Kendall said before dashing from the room.

Ian immediately jumped up and slapping me on the shoulder said, "I would never have seen that coming."

I looked at him like he'd gone crazy. "What is so far-fetched about me dating Kendall?" I said defensively.

"Well, I'm just surprised, is all," he said shrugging.

I was just about to demand an explanation when the nurse came out to give us an update. "Mr. O'Neal has been taken up to room 317. You can all go up now."

Kendall walked up just as I was going to go looking for her. She'd gotten everyone coffee and I took the tray giving her a sincere "Thank you." She gave me a tender smile and I explained we were going to be able to go up to see my dad.

"Well, I'll wait for you here," she said getting ready to sit down.

"No, Kendall. I want you to meet my dad. Please." I handed the coffee to Ian who was standing by watching us closely and held out my hand to her.

She took my hand and softly said, "I'd like that."

We took a silent ride to the third floor and as we approached my dad's room, we could see his physician,

Dr. Lumsden in deep conversation with the nurse on duty. He looked up as we approached, signed a chart he'd been holding and with a sympathetic smile, asked us to join him in the family room.

When we'd all gotten seated, the doctor sat across from us and opening a folder, directed his conversation to my mom. "Katie…I think you should know that we're on the final leg of Patrick's journey. We've known this day was coming but truthfully, I'm surprised at how quickly it's come."

My mom nodded while twisting a piece of tissue with her hands fretfully. "I've seen it happening, I just can't seem to accept it."

He took a deep breath and blew it out. "We're making him comfortable but I think if you've got anything to say to him, now is the time. He's not going to be very coherent if we have to put him on morphine for pain. I want you to have some quality conversation with him before that happens."

He stood and took my mom's hand. "He needs to know you're all here." We walked down the hallway to his room and he glanced over when we came in. I'd expected a room full of machines but he just had a couple of IV poles next his bed. His eyes lit up when he saw my mom.

"Katie, darlin'," he said holding out his hand to her. She rushed forward to kiss him on the forehead.

"Patrick, I'm sorry we didn't get in here sooner. They had us wait in the lobby," she said trailing her fingers down his cheek.

My dad smiled at her with such love that I had to take a deep breath to keep my emotions in check. I looked over at Ian and saw he was struggling just as hard as I was. He glanced at me and gave me a slight nod of acknowledgment.

After a moment, dad focused on Kendall. "Well, who is this beautiful young lady, Tristan?" He asked, holding out a trembling hand to her.

"Dad, this is Kendall." She reached out and took his hand and he pulled her closer to him.

"I'm so glad I got to meet you. Tristan said you were very special," he said, fighting to keep his eyes open. The nurse came in and adjusted his medication while checking to make sure he was comfortable.

Kendall's chin was trembling as she fought back tears. "I'm glad I could be here."

My dad struggled to stay awake. "Boys, I want to talk to each of you alone for a moment."

I gestured for Ian to go first, and I walked my mom and Kendall out into the hallway to wait. I wrapped my arm around Mom and held Kendall's hand tightly. A few moments passed, and Ian came out wiping his puffy red eyes. "You're next, Tristan," he said as he gathered mom into his arms.

Releasing Kendall's hand, I stepped back into dad's room. I could tell this was exhausting him, and I felt my heart break at the thought of him suffering. He smiled weakly as I sat down next to the bed and he held his hand out to me. I grasped it with both of mine and pressed my forehead to his hand. "Son, look at me." he rasped.

I lifted my head to find his eyes were clear and coherent, something they hadn't been in a long time. "Yes, Dad?" I managed to say without losing it.

"I want you to know that I love you and am so proud of the man you've become." He took a labored breath. "There's so much I want to say but I don't have the strength. Son, I need you to take good care of your mother. She's going to need you and your brother more than ever." He paused again to take a deep ragged breath. "I want you to promise me that you will."

Suddenly, the reality of everything came crashing down on me. "Dad," I said as my voice was breaking, "I don't want to lose you."

"Son, it's out of our hands," he said softly.

I choked back the tears as I said, "Dad, I promise I'll take good care of mom."

He studied my face for a moment then spoke so softly that I struggled to hear him. "I pray you find the love of your life like I did. You deserve it, Tristan."

Tears spilled down my cheeks as I squeezed his hand and said, "Dad, I hope I'm half the man you are."

He smiled, his eyes fluttering shut. "I'm so tired, please send your mom in, Son."

I reluctantly stood as I was wiping the tears streaming down my face. Opening the door and standing in the doorway, I saw my mom look over at me with tear-filled eyes. "He wants you, Mom." I managed to say. She unwrapped herself from Ian's embrace and as she passed me, she cupped my face and gave me a sweet smile. Silently, she turned and entered the room shutting the door behind her.

Kendall was leaning against the window, her arms wrapped around herself, gazing out into the darkness. As I walked up, she turned to look at me and I could see she'd been crying. I took her into my arms and we just held each other, no words were needed. We stood quietly knowing this was probably the end. A few minutes passed and we saw a nurse go into the room followed by the doctor. Ian's eyes met mine and I felt a sinking feeling in my gut. The door opened and they both came out, stood speaking quietly for a moment and then the doctor came over to us. I knew what he was going to say before he said it but when he said, "He's gone," it felt like someone had punched me in the stomach. I closed my eyes as I let out a ragged breath. I felt Kendall let me go and saw Ian coming over to me with a lost look in his eyes. I pulled him into a tight hug and felt his shoulders shake with each sob.

The doctor was still standing close by giving us time to absorb the news. "If you would like to go in one last time, you're welcome to do so."

Ian's eyes looked at me wildly. "I can't see him like that Tristan!" He said backing away.

I grabbed his arm before he took off. "You don't have to. He's just giving us the time to do it, if we want. Mom's sitting in there by herself…I'll go make sure she's okay."

He nodded and went to sit in one of the chairs in the family waiting room. I watched as Kendall slowly made her way over to him, sat down beside him and put her arm around his shoulders. Her eyes met mine as I started to go into the room. I smiled and mouthed *thank you.* Wiping her eyes, she nodded and sat next to Ian giving him silent support.

Chapter 10

Kendall

After Tristan and Katie came out of the hospital room, I could see the pain on their faces and it brought back the flood of memories from the loss of my parents and sister. Tristan didn't say a word, just came over and hugged me tightly again and told me he needed to make the arrangements. I walked over and sat with his mom and that was when I noticed Ian was gone.

"Kendall," Katie began, "thank you for being here with us tonight." She dabbed at her eyes with a tissue. "I'm so glad you got to meet Patrick."

I took her hand and held it until Tristan came back with some paperwork. "Mom, it's all taken care of. Let's get you home."

We stood and I saw her take one last look at the hospital room door. "I can't believe he's gone," she said to Tristan. "I've known this day was coming for a while but it didn't make it any easier."

He put his arm around her and took my hand and we walked out of the hospital. Tristan drove me home first, explaining that he'd probably be staying at his mom's for a couple of nights to help take care of things and make sure she was okay. When he dropped me off, he asked me if I'd go with him to the memorial service, and I told him I'd be honored. He told me he'd call me and give me the information about the service. "Tristan, I'll meet you there, you'll need to ride with your mom in the family car. I can come by myself."

Taking a deep breath, he nodded. "Thanks for being with me tonight. You've no idea how much it means to me."

He gave me a quick kiss and was gone.

I dragged up the stairs and once inside my apartment, threw myself on the bed and called Averi.

"Hey! What's up? I haven't heard from you in a few days," she said cheerily.

"A lot's been going on," I managed to say before breaking down.

"Kendall, I'll be right over." The phone went dead, and I threw it down beside me on the bed.

About fifteen minutes later, Averi rang the bell, and I dragged myself down the stairs to let her in. "You look terrible," she said as she looked me up and down. "What's going on?"

"Tristan's dad passed away just a little while ago."

Her eyes grew wide. "Oh that's terrible. Was it sudden?"

Shaking my head, I said, "No, he had cancer."

"Oh Kendall, I'm sure that was torture for his family. Are they okay?"

I felt tears welling up, and I managed a shrug. "As well as can be expected."

She placed her hand on my shoulder. "Well, tell them if they need anything, please let me know."

"I will. Thanks for coming over. I just needed to talk to someone. This has brought back all the memories of what happened to my family, and I feel a little freaked out. I finally told Tristan about my family and the fire."

Averi nodded. "I can see you're freaked. Look Kendall, you never got to say goodbye and seeing Tristan and his family go through something where they were able to come to terms with a death probably has kicked you in the gut."

I looked at her with surprise. "That's exactly how I feel right now. Like someone kicked me right in the gut."

She nodded with understanding. "That's perfectly normal. If you didn't care, you wouldn't feel a thing. So, are you going to the memorial?" She asked.

"Tristan asked me to. I think I should," I answered with a sigh.

"I think you should too and let yourself experience all the grief you didn't show when your family died." She grabbed a tissue from the box and handed it to me. "You've got to deal with this someday and maybe you're meant to share it with Tristan. You can help each other."

Taking a deep breath, I nodded. "You're right. I have to go."

She stood up and pulled me up to give me a hug. "I love you Kendall. You're going to be okay. I gotta run but call me tomorrow, okay? I'm going to try to make it but I have to work."

I nodded and walked her down to the front door. "Goodnight Averi, I love you, too."

Tristan called me the next morning and told me the memorial was set for the following day. His dad's wishes were to be cremated so they were going to have a "Celebration of Life" memorial in his honor.

I went through the motions at work but was always thinking about Tristan. I knew it had to be hard taking care of things while grieving, I'd been there myself.

The day of the memorial began with bright sunshine, and I picked out a beautiful sun dress in navy blue to wear. Averi called to check on me, and I told her I was trying to be strong, for Tristan. I left Becky in charge of the store for a couple of hours, so I could go. As I walked into the chapel, I saw Tristan's eyes scanning the room until they met mine. He smiled, and I felt my heart melt at seeing him again. He excused himself from the conversation he was having and made his way over to me. "Kendall," he said pulling me into a tight hug. "I've missed you. Come sit with us…please?" He gestured to the family section, and I balked for a moment but saw this was important to him. Katie rose when she saw me and grabbed my hand pulling me over to sit beside her. Ian was sitting somberly at the end of the row sparing me a glance as I sat down.

Before the service began, I glanced around the room and was pleased to see so many of the locals among the crowd. Tristan sat next to me and held my hand tightly. He absently rubbed his thumb across my hand. The minister stood and began the service, and I listened to him honor Patrick James O'Neal. Katie gazed wistfully at the picture on the cover of the program she held in her hand of her smiling husband. After the formal service, the minister invited everyone to join the family for refreshments and some visitation time. Tristan held onto my hand as we entered the fellowship hall of the church where they had some refreshments set up and friends and family were mingling. I scanned the room to see if Averi was able to make it away from work in time but instead saw Logan Walker staring in my direction with a strange look on his face. I looked around to see what he was looking at and realized it was me he was focused on. His strange expression morphed into a smirk and he turned and was gone. Tristan introduced me to some family friends and soon I forgot about Logan. Averi showed up and I introduced her to Tristan's mom. I saw Ian watching her as she spoke with some of the others in the room until finally she ended up right in front of him. "I'm sorry for your loss," she said holding out her hand.

Ian hesitated then took her hand. "Thank you for coming," he said with a sad smile. Their eyes stayed locked together as they both said nothing more. Finally, he looked as if he were about to say something when someone came up to introduce him to a visitor and Averi quietly slipped away. After seeing their encounter, I knew there had to be a mutual attraction that they were both denying.

After about an hour of mingling, it was time to go. I gave Katie a hug and emphasized if she needed anything to please let me know. Tristan pulled me into a hug and whispered, "I miss you."

"I miss you, too," I said softly. "Take care of your mom. I'll be around."

He nodded, kissed me gently and walked his mom out to the waiting family car. Ian gave me a slight nod as he followed them out.

I went home, climbed into bed and cried myself to sleep thinking about their family's loss as well as my own.

The nightmare returned that night. Once again, I was running through the yard, my legs like lead, keeping me from getting there in time. I relived the fireman grabbing me and was about to scream when my alarm went off. My heart was pounding, and I was panting like I'd actually been running. I sat up in my bed trying to compose myself and after sleep eluded me further, I decided to go downstairs and do some baking to calm my nerves.

It was still early, but I knew George would be in as usual so I unlocked the door, put the coffee on and went into the kitchen to start some muffins. I heard the jingle of the doorbell not long after and I yelled out, "George, there's fresh coffee on, help yourself. I'm putting some muffins in now."

I slid the muffin pan in the oven and realized I hadn't heard a response. "George?" I called out as I came from the kitchen.

Thick muscular arms grabbed me from behind before I realized what was happening. They wrapped around me like a vise holding my wrists crossed in front of me. I started to scream but the man growled, "Make a noise and this'll get ugly. You understand? Nod if you understand."

Panic-stricken, I nodded, my heart thundering in my chest. He dragged me into the kitchen, and as he did, he spun me around into the wall, knocking the breath out of me. Before I could recover, he had his forearm at my throat holding me tightly against the wall. I could now see his face, and I felt all the blood drain from my own. Logan Walker's face was inches from mine and from the smell of his breath, he'd been drinking.

"Well, well. Kendall darlin'. It's time you and I had a talk," he growled menacingly.

I was seeing spots from how tightly he was pressing on my throat, and I clawed at his arm trying to get him to let me breathe. He looked confused for a moment then eased the pressure enough to let me catch my breath. "What do you want?" I managed to croak out.

He sneered as he leaned even closer, pressing his body suggestively against mine. "Seems you've been whoring around on my good buddy, Sebastian. He told me all about you and him being together so, when I saw you yesterday, I just had to ask him if he knew you were seeing Tristan. He was pretty torn up about it and since you'd slammed me in front of my friends at the bonfire, I was more than happy to volunteer to give you a message from him."

Still struggling to breathe, I managed to hiss, "I'm not his property and we are not together!"

He scoffed, "Bitch, say what you want but I know there's something going on with you two. He said to remind you that nobody's safe, your family, your friends, especially Tristan. He has his phone number and has followed him home so if you don't want something bad to happen to him, you'd better break it off."

I felt tears welling in my eyes. "Please… please tell him not to hurt anyone," I begged.

He buried his face in my neck and took a deep breath. "I'll tell him but in the meantime, I think you owe me something…something I've wanted for a long time."

I felt his free hand fumbling to untie my apron and fear gripped me. I had no way to fight him, the hold he had on my neck was making me dizzy and sapping my strength. His breath was hot against my skin and before I could react, his mouth came brutally crashing down on mine. I could taste blood as his mouth ground my lip against my teeth. Tears streamed freely down my cheeks as he rubbed himself against me, his hand now sliding up my shirt. "I've been wanting to do this for a long time," he growled. "Sebastian doesn't need to know about this, you understand? This can be our little secret."

I closed my eyes as he moved his forearm from my throat only to replace it with his hand. I felt myself begin to sway, consciousness leaving me and I knew if I passed out, there was no telling what he would do. As I was blacking out, I heard the jingle of the doorbell. Suddenly, he froze. Then I heard the sweetest voice call out, "Kendall?" Thank God, it was George.

Still holding me against the wall, Logan hissed, "This ain't over, darlin'." He let me go then shoved me before he dashed out my back door.

"Kendall, you okay?" George said coming a little closer to the kitchen.

I attempted to clear my throat which was raw like it was on fire. "Yes, George…" I said gruffly. "I just finished some muffins. Be out in a minute." I was surprised at how calm I sounded.

"Okay, I hope you're not coming down with something. You sound terrible. I'm pouring myself a cup of coffee. I'll take one of those muffins when they're done."

"I woke up with a scratchy throat. I'm sure it's nothing, though. Help yourself to the coffee," I said attempting to sound normal. Inside I was totally freaking out. If George hadn't shown up, there was no telling what Logan would've done. Sebastian was dangerous and now with Logan involved, they had their sights set on my family, friends and Tristan. I went into the bathroom and washed my face noticing I had a split lip and my neck was already bruising from Logan's choke hold. I quickly ran upstairs and grabbed a pretty scarf which I wrapped loosely around my neck before going back downstairs.

Becky was in the kitchen taking the muffins out of the oven when I came in and she smiled. Her smile quickly faded as she saw my lip. "What in the world did you do, Kendall?"

I laughed, "Oh, this?" I said shaking my head while I threw my hands up. "I walked into the bathroom door. I'm such a klutz."

She joined in the laughter. "I do those crazy things too. My husband swears I'm an accident waiting to happen."

I smiled and grabbed a couple of muffins out of the pan and took them out to George. He was seated in his usual spot reading the newspaper and he smiled when he saw me coming, but his smile quickly faded. "Kendall, is everything okay? What did you do to your lip?"

Unconsciously, my hand went to the scarf at my throat. "Oh, I ran into the bathroom door, I'll be okay. I was just telling Becky what a klutz I was," I said resting my hand on his shoulder. He seemed to accept my explanation, and I went back to work.

The rest of the day was busy and when the last person had gone and I'd locked the front door, I went up to my apartment and as I closed the door, the flood of emotions I'd kept bottled up all day burst forth. I threw myself on my bed sobbing into my pillow. I heard my phone chime with a text and with tear-filled eyes saw it was from Tristan.

Hey baby, just thinking of you.

With my heart breaking, I knew what I had to do.

Tristan, please don't contact me anymore. I've been lying to you and it's time to stop. I've been seeing someone else and we're serious. I've made my choice so please just leave me alone.

I hesitated, my finger over the send button. As a tear ran down my cheek, I tapped the screen and the message was gone.

I turned off my phone and with tears streaming from my eyes, I curled into a ball and lay sleepless until the sun came up.

The next morning, I turned on my phone and saw several messages from Tristan which I promptly deleted. I couldn't bear to read them knowing they were full of confusion and possibly anger. This way was best. Breaking it off with him was going to save the people I loved from harm and that was most important. I opened the store and went through my day trying to stay busy to keep my mind off of Tristan and how I was hurting him. I saw Averi coming in to get her morning coffee and I quickly told Becky I had to run up to my apartment. I hid until she'd left, and I was ashamed that I was forced to hide, but I knew Averi wouldn't accept the klutz story, and I had to avoid seeing her until my bruises healed. Once again I checked my phone and saw more messages from Tristan and again, I deleted them without reading them. Common sense told me this was for the best but it was breaking my heart. At the end of the day, after everyone had left and I'd locked up, I walked over to my bedroom window and threw it open to let in the sea breeze. That was when I saw him. Sebastian was down below on the boardwalk smoking a cigarette. He looked up and saw me immediately and stood glaring, his message clear. I backed away from the window collapsing onto my bed. This nightmare was real and it was never going to end. The ringing of my doorbell startled me and with my heart thumping, I ran down the stairs stopping in the shadows to see who was there. In the twilight, I could just make out Averi's face pressed up against the glass. "Kendall, let me in!" She yelled pounding her fist on the door.

I walked down the last few steps and threw open the door. "What?" I asked abruptly, glancing around to make sure Sebastian wasn't lurking near the door.

She looked at me and gasped. "What in the hell happened to you?" She demanded pushing her way in the door pointing at my now bare neck. I threw my hand up to cover myself but she grabbed my arm and wouldn't let me. "It's worse than I thought," she said flipping on the light. "George told me your lame story about walking into the door, which he didn't believe, by the way."

"Everyone needs to mind their own business," I muttered holding my chin down to hide the bruises on my neck.

Averi shook her head. "No, that's not going to happen. Did Tristan do this to you?"

"No!" I said shocked. "Tristan would never hurt me. I walked into the door. End of discussion."

"So, the door grabbed you by the throat leaving finger marks?" She asked as she examined me more closely.

I took a deep breath, then sighed before answering, "Averi, just leave it alone. For the sake of everyone I love, including you, leave it alone."

She frowned. "Kendall, we've been friends for too long for you to ask me to do that. I can't stand to see you like this. I'm here for you, whatever it is." She paused. "Well since you say he didn't do this, has Tristan seen you? What did he say? Did he believe the 'I ran into the door' story?"

"I'm not seeing him anymore."

"WHAT?" She cried. "What in the world is going on? The other day you were inseparable and now you're not seeing him? Did he break up with you?"

I sighed. "No, I broke up with him. I can't see him. It's best for everyone."

"Kendall, I'm at a loss. You're like a stranger to me right now." She paced back and forth in front of me gesturing in the air with her hands. "You just threw away the one man you truly loved. I can't comprehend this."

She shook her head in disbelief. When I didn't respond, she continued, "Does this have anything to do with Mr. Creepy himself, Sebastian? I've noticed him lurking around here a lot lately." When I didn't respond, she stopped pacing and stopped right in front of me. "Does it?" She persisted.

"Averi, I'll ask you again to leave it alone."

She nodded almost imperceptibly. "Sure, sure. I'll leave it alone." I could see tears welling in her eyes. "I love you too much to lose you again."

A single tear fell from my eye as I grabbed her and hugged her tightly. "And I love you. You mean the world to me and I'd do anything for you…anything."

Chapter 11

Tristan

It had been several days since the breakup text from Kendall and despite my messages, I hadn't heard a thing back from her. I was sitting at my desk going back over everything in my mind and couldn't bring myself to believe she'd been lying to me. I'd told my mom about the whole thing and she'd been as surprised as I was. She kept saying over and over that didn't sound like the Kendall she knew. My thoughts were interrupted by my assistant on the intercom. "Mr. O'Neal, your brother is here to see you."

I hadn't seen Ian since the memorial service. He'd disappeared only checking in with mom by text claiming he needed some alone time to think. "Send him in, Jerica."

The door opened and Ian came shuffling in dressed in clothes that looked like they'd been slept in for days.

He had dark circles under his eyes, his hair was all mussed up and he looked like he hadn't shaved. "Hey," he said before dropping into a chair in front of my desk.

"Hey, yourself. Where have you been?" I leaned back in my chair and waited for the elaborate excuse.

He hesitated then just shrugged. "I've been staying with Pops and his wife on their couch."

"Pops? You mean Hoby? What were you doing there?" I leaned forward folding my arms on the desk.

He rubbed his forehead. "Well, I just needed to go somewhere and they've always been nice to me. I know I hurt mom and disappointed you but I just needed time to think. I'm sorry."

This wasn't the arrogant Ian I knew. He looked broken and the grief he was feeling was palpable. I studied him then got up and walked over to his chair and put my hand on his shoulder. "Ian, I'm not disappointed. Hurt, maybe…but not disappointed. And as for mom, she loves you and apparently understands you more than I do. She told me she knew you'd be okay and you'd come back when you were ready."

He looked up at me and grinned. "I'll go by and see her in a little while. I need to go home and clean up first."

I laughed. "Yeah, I think that's a good idea." Walking over to my desk, I perched on the edge and folded my arms over my chest. "So, you're ready to join the world again?"

He nodded. "Yeah, I think so."

"Well good, because you've got a job here. They told me this morning and I said I'd give you the good news."

He broke into a huge smile. "Really? That's awesome! When do I start?"

"How's Monday sound? You'll be working with Mrs. Hawley in the loan department to start. It's entry level but I'm sure you'll move up in no time. I've also heard she's a great person to work with so I think you'll be okay."

"That sounds great! I tell you what…I'll take you and Kendall out for dinner to celebrate when I get my first paycheck."

"Well, that's going to be a problem. Kendall and I aren't seeing each other anymore," I said feeling the need to straighten some papers on my desk.

Eyebrows raised, he barraged me with questions. "What? When did this happen? You were together just a few days ago! What did you do?"

I shrugged. "I have no idea. Everything was fine and then I got the breakup text."

He appeared puzzled. "She broke up with you by text? She doesn't seem like that type of person. Even in school she was always nice, quiet but nice. I wasn't always nice to her but that's another story."

"Wait, what? She went to school with you?"

"Bro, she went to school with both of us. That's why I was so surprised that you were dating her. She was 'different' in school and didn't seem like your type."

I closed my eyes trying to picture her. "I can't remember her…you'd think I'd remember someone as stunning as her."

"Well," he laughed, "she didn't exactly look the same as she does now. Let's just say, she was one of the kids who blended in. Plus, you were dating Maria and probably couldn't see beyond that."

I sat there trying to picture Kendall and suddenly it hit me. I knew there was something familiar about her when I first saw her but couldn't put my finger on it. She had fallen into my arms in the hallway that day and for that moment, I'd found myself looking into the most beautiful blue eyes I'd ever seen. She'd disappeared as soon as I'd steadied her and after that, I'd looked for her but never saw her again. With time, the memory had faded but now it was perfectly clear. "Do you think she remembers me from school?" I asked out loud before answering my own question. "Nah, probably not. When I told her I went to school here, she never mentioned it."

Ian looked at me as if I'd lost my mind. "Really? Don't you get it, Tristan? You were one of the popular kids, she wasn't in your league. She probably knew exactly who you were but didn't want you to figure out who she was."

Suddenly, I felt ashamed. "Was I that damn stuck up? I never thought of myself as above anyone and now you tell me I was in a different league than Kendall! I can't believe I was so blind. I missed out on spending time with one of the most beautiful souls I've ever met because of social status."

Ian nodded. "I know your pain. I've had my eye on Averi since high school too but she's always looked down on me, and I totally understand it. I've been an ass, sleeping around to prove something to myself, I guess. All it did was kill any chance I had to be with her."

I shook my head. "Boy we are a couple of winners, aren't we? The two women we want more than anything, don't want anything to do with us."

Ian chuckled. "Well, we can either accept that and move on or we can keep trying. What do you think?"

I closed my eyes and Kendall's face came to mind. "I think I love her, Ian. I really do."

"Well, then we need to figure out some way to fix this. Since you're on Kendall's do not call list, I think I'll do some snooping around and see what's up with her. You do some scouting for me with Averi."

I stood up and held out my hand. "Sounds like a plan, brother!" He shook my hand and grinned. "Okay, get out of here, go get cleaned up and over to see mom. She's missed you."

Grinning sheepishly, he turned to walk out of my office. As he got to the door, he turned to look back at me. "I know I don't say it enough but thanks for everything you've done for me."

I returned the grin. "That's what brothers are for."

After he left, I sat down and looked up the number for the henna shop. I started to dial the number but stopped midway through. This wasn't the type of conversation to have on the phone. This needed to be a face to face conversation. I finished the rest of the paperwork on my desk and was just about to leave for the day when Jerica buzzed me. "Mr. O'Neal, you have a phone call. He won't give me his name. He says you'll know who he is."

I picked up the phone and heard a familiar voice. "Tristan! How goes life at the beach?"

"Great Jay! How goes life in the mountains?" I said laughing.

"Awesome! You left before we got the good news…Jane's expecting! We're going to have a little girl. Jolene's so excited that she's going to be a big sister."

"Congratulations to you both! Oh and please tell Jolene I said hello. I'll never forget she thought I was a prince," I said chuckling.

He laughed along with me. "Sure will! Hey, we have a couple of questions about the project that apparently you took notes for. Can I e-mail those over to you and you take a look?"

"Absolutely! I don't mind at all. By the way, anytime you guys are headed this way, give me a call. I'd love to catch up."

"Sounds good. We probably won't make it this summer but definitely after baby Olivia gets here we'll be in need of a vacation. I'll give you a call. Keep in touch, okay?"

"Olivia, huh? Nice name. You broke the 'J' tradition though, man!" I said laughing.

He laughed heartily. "Oh you don't know how hard that was. We tossed around Jodi, Jennifer, Jessica and Judy but Jolene looked at us and said matter-offactly, 'Her name's Olivia.' Apparently, there's a mouse in one of her Disney movies named Olivia and since she picked Ryder's name, we thought, why not."

I couldn't help but smile remembering how adorable Jolene was. "Well, you've got two beautiful ladies in your life and one more on the way. You're a lucky man, Jay."

"Yeah, I have to agree. Well, I'm going to get that e-mail over to you. Take care and keep in touch!"

"Sounds good! I've still got the same e-mail so I'll be looking for it and get it back to you as soon as possible. Take care and give Jane my best."

"Will do! Bye for now!"

I hung the phone up still smiling. Jay and Jane had been so nice to me when I worked on the new bank building project for Mr. Davenport. They were a perfect couple, and I felt a twinge of envy. I wanted a future with Kendall. I wanted to know the excitement of having a child with someone you love. I had to do something and the time was now.

I jumped in my Jeep, drove home and threw on some shorts and a t-shirt. I drove to the boardwalk and rather than park in the parking lot right beside it, I parked down the street. I saw a group of people walking down the boardwalk so I attached myself to their group breaking off when I got to the henna shop. Averi was working when I walked in and she glanced up and her eyes grew wide as her mouth fell open. I wandered around looking at the various souvenirs for sale and heard her finish up with her client with her 'Don't smear this' warning. The young woman left the shop and Averi came right over to me.

"First of all," she began, "I can't tell you any more than you already know."

I held up my hands. "Whoa. What do you think I'm doing here? Stalking Kendall?"

She seemed embarrassed. "Uh, no! I just thought you might've come in search of answers. Answers I don't have."

I sighed. "Truthfully, I am trying to get answers. I don't understand the sudden change in her feelings for me. She sent me a text telling me that she'd been seeing someone all along and that they were serious and she needed to stop lying and let me go."

The shocked expression on Averi's face proved to me something wasn't right. "She told you WHAT?" She said frowning.

"She was seeing someone and it was serious," I repeated.

She shook her head. "That's not true. She's hiding something and I don't know what. She said breaking up with you was for the best…for everyone. I tried to get her to tell me but she wouldn't. And the bru—" She stopped short of finishing. "Never mind."

"Averi, could you do me a favor and just watch out for her? I've tried sending her messages and I can only hope she's reading them but I don't know. I really care about her and want to be with her."

She nodded. "I'm definitely watching out for her and I believe you. I honestly think you're the best thing that's ever happened to her."

"Thanks. Oh! Hey, did she know that we went to school together? I mean, did she know who I was?" I asked.

The flush on her face told me the answer before she even began speaking. "If I told you the truth, she'd kill me."

"Please, Averi. I need to know if there was something there…ever."

She hesitated then walked over to sit on the stool. "Have a seat. I think it's time to let you in on the history." I sat in the chair opposite her and leaning back in her chair, she began. "Tristan, Kendall's been in love with you since she was in ninth grade and you were a senior. One day, she got pushed by an asshole football jock and you caught her before she fell on the floor and that was when she fell and fell hard…for you. She told me this story a couple of years after it happened when we were both confessing…um…well suffice to say, she spilled the beans to me about the first time she saw you."

I sat there in stunned silence, again remembering that day and how mad I'd been at Trey for pushing her and being a jerk. She'd fallen into my arms so easily, and I remembered asking if she was okay.

Averi continued. "She's been through a lot, Tristan. I know she's told you about her family dying in a fire, but there's more to the story that she's not telling…I can feel it. I may be her best friend but she's keeping secrets from me and it has to be behind the reason she broke it off with you."

I nodded. "She's opened up to me only a little and honestly, I didn't press the issue. It was obviously still very painful for her."

"Well, all I know is that the fire was suspicious and the investigators questioned her about it but found she hadn't been anywhere near the house at the time. She and I weren't speaking when this happened, we'd drifted apart. After the fire, she came to live with my family and me for a couple of weeks then moved into the apartment over the store. Her grandparents wanted her to come to live with them but she'd made up her mind to work in the store and take night classes to finish school."

"So, she never said where she'd been the night of the fire?" I asked.

"No. I've never asked, either."

I stood up to leave. "Thank you for talking with me. I don't know why she's running from me but I'm not going to give up that easily."

Averi stood up. "Good luck, Tristan. She's worth it." I gave her a hug, and I left the shop and blended in with the crowds on the boardwalk. I wandered out onto the beach and could see the front of Kendall's store and the people going in and out. I saw George come out and stroll slowly down the boardwalk, and then I noticed the guy I'd seen on the boardwalk after my date with Kendall leaning up against the railing near her store. He appeared to be watching the place and it gave me an uneasy feeling. He'd said he was from out of town but now that I could see him in the light, something about him was familiar. I was trying to remember what he'd said his name was when I heard a shout.

"Yo, Tristan!" I heard my name and turned to see Hoby jogging up the beach. He stopped, taking a moment to catch his breath then said, "You going surfing later? We've got a tropical storm coming up the coast and it's going to be throwing up some great waves."

I shrugged slipping my hands in my pockets. "I don't know, not really in the surfing mood. Hey, do you happen to know that guy up on the boardwalk?" I said pointing at the mystery creeper.

He peered up at the boardwalk and nodded. "Sure, that's Sebastian Cole. He's trouble, been that way since he was in high school. He was one of those kids who was always in trouble for breaking and entering. I had to call the law a couple of times about him trying to break in my storage building."

I listened in disbelief. "So he grew up around here? That's odd, he told me he wasn't from here."

"That is strange. Yeah, he went to school with you guys...you probably wouldn't have hung around with his crowd though. I'd heard Kendall was hanging out with him for a while but after the fire, the word was that she'd left all that behind to run her parent's store."

This was all good information that I needed to know. "So, you knew about the fire, too? Apparently, I was living in Charlotte when it happened."

He nodded somberly. "Yeah, that was tragic. Three lives lost in an instant and they never did find a cause for it." I glanced at Sebastian and saw he'd been joined by Logan Walker. I knew Logan vaguely from school, he'd been on the football team with Ian, and now seeing him again, I recognized him as the guy hassling Kendall at the bonfire. They seemed to be in a serious conversation and they were both looking at Kendall's store. Hoby looked up at them and shook his head. "I guess trouble loves trouble. Logan got banned from the beach after the last bonfire. He showed up drunk and started a fight with Colin Burns. Colin had some of his EMT buddies with him and they put him face down in the sand. He seems to be on a downhill slide lately." We watched as they shook hands and Sebastian walked away leaving Logan behind in his place. A few minutes later, I saw a police officer who'd been patrolling the boardwalk walk up to him and after a brief conversation, Logan left. The entire situation was giving me a bad feeling but there wasn't anything I could do. Kendall had made that clear.

Hoby placed his hand on my shoulder. "I don't know what's going on, but I'd keep an eye on Kendall. If either of those creeps has their eye on her then she's not safe."

I nodded. "I agree and you know I will."

Chapter 11

Kendall

Days passed and my wounds were healing but inside my heart was breaking. Also, my fear of Sebastian and Logan was growing. It seemed that every time I looked outside, one or the other was lurking out on the boardwalk. They had me trapped like I was in prison, and I had no one to help me escape. In order to protect the ones I loved, I had to live this way. Averi had come by a couple of times but only stayed for a few minutes. I missed her and most of all, I missed Tristan. I'd lay in bed at night and remember the time we'd spent together. It had been a dream come true, and I would always treasure that glimpse of what my life could have been. George and Becky had noticed my depression and tried to talk to me about it, but I just said that I wasn't seeing Tristan anymore, and I didn't want to talk about it. I could feel their eyes following me as I went about my daily routine, but I put on my best fake smile and made my way through each day.

One day after work, I looked out and saw my guards were missing from the boardwalk. Dying to get out, I locked up the store and made my way down to the beach. It was low tide and the surf was quiet compared to the violent waves that had been stirred up by the tropical storm we'd had recently. I walked into the ocean letting it rush across my feet, the sensation of the bubbling water soothing to my soul. The sea breeze ruffled my hair, and I took a deep cleansing breath as I stretched my arms over my head reaching for the sky. I gazed out at the horizon and suddenly felt a presence behind me. "So my bird has flown from her cage?" I turned to see Sebastian standing a few feet back, his arms crossed in front of him. "The one time I don't have someone watching you…"

I turned to face him. "You don't have to watch me night and day. I broke it off with Tristan, as you commanded," I said through clenched teeth.

He took a step toward me and that's when I realized the beach was empty except for us. "Kendall, why do you make it sound that way. I just need you to keep your mouth shut. I can't afford for you to spill all our secrets while you're in bed with him. Besides, I want you for myself."

My skin crawled at the thought of him touching me. "Sebastian, our arrangement didn't include me being your property."

He moved closer as I took a step back. "I've dreamed of being with you. Surely you always knew how I felt."

"We were friends, Sebastian, nothing more. I thought you knew that, I thought you understood that." I felt the waves splashing higher on my legs and realized I'd slowly stepped backward. "If I ever gave you the impression it was any more, then I'm sorry. My heart has always belonged to someone else."

He spit out, "That damn Tristan. He's so perfect, is he? Did you sleep with him, Kendall? If you did, I'm going to be very, very angry."

Keeping my emotions in check, I answered, "If you must know, no. We enjoyed each other's company but we didn't go that far." No matter what I didn't need Tristan to be a target.

"Good," he said smirking. "I don't want another man touching you."

My encounter with Logan flashed through my mind but again, the fear of violence kept my mouth shut. "He didn't, no one has."

"He'd better not. I know where he lives. You don't want him getting hurt, do you, Kendall?"

I shook my head as tears welled in my eyes. "Please don't…" I whispered.

He stepped into the water and took me by the arm pulling me back on shore. I didn't fight him knowing that it would just make things worse. I stood stiffly as he wrapped his arms around me. "Mmm, you smell so good," he said burying his face in the crook of my neck. "I'll have you one day, Kendall. It's inevitable."

"Hey, Kendall!" As I heard my name, I heard Sebastian sigh with irritation. He looked up and growled, "Be cool."

I turned to see Stacy holding hands with a little girl. "Hi, Stacy," I managed to say, keeping my voice steady. "How've you been?"

She smiled. "Pretty good…Kendall, this is my little sister Emily." She looked at Sebastian with curiosity. "Um, hi." Nodding mutely, he kept his arm around me tightly, possessively.

After an uncomfortable silence, she said, "Well, we'd better be going. It's getting dark."

I nodded as I felt Sebastian squeeze me tighter. "You have a good night," I said evenly. "Nice to meet you, Emily." They walked away, and I felt helpless and alone. Sebastian moved closer again, and I knew what he wanted by the look in his eye. I was running out of options and time.

"Kendall!" Thank God, it was Averi! She came running down the boardwalk looking over the railing. "Kendall, is that you?"

"Damn it!" Sebastian cursed. "Is this some kind of conspiracy?" He grabbed me by both arms, his face inches from mine. "I'm going to let you go for tonight but this isn't over. Just remember, we have an understanding."

He pushed me away and jogged away disappearing quickly into the shadows under the boardwalk. I turned to see Averi and Ian come running down the beach toward me. "Are you okay?" She asked looking around to see if I was alone. "Stacy called me and told me to get my ass down here. She said you looked like you needed saving."

"Yeah, I'm okay." I looked curiously at Ian. Averi looked at him, then at me. "Oh, I happened to see Ian trolling for women on the boardwalk and grabbed him."

I saw Ian shake his head. "Trolling? Really, Little Bit? I was going down to the surf shop to get some wax."

Averi waved her hand as if dismissing him. "Ian, you're always trolling. You can say what you want, but I'm just glad you happened to be passing by my door when you were." Turning her attention back to me, she said, "So, who were you with just a minute ago? Stacy said she thought she recognized the guy but wasn't sure. She said you looked really uncomfortable."

I hated to lie but what was another one thrown on the pile I'd already thrown out lately. "It was a friend," I responded. "He asked me to meet him down here so we could be alone."

Suddenly, shame came flooding over me as I realized what I'd just said in front of Tristan's brother. His eyes snapped up to meet mine. "So, there's someone else? To be honest, I didn't see you as that type. Guess you fooled Tristan, huh?"

"How is he?" I whispered.

He threw his hands up and shook his head. "He's pretty damn confused, to be perfectly honest."

Unable to meet his eyes that were so much like Tristan's, I turned toward the ocean where I could barely make out the horizon in the dying light. "I'm sorry. I know that really doesn't make it better but I'm afraid…I can't say any more."

"Well, that's just great," he said sarcastically. "I'm glad you're sorry. My brother's an awesome guy and deserved better than a text breaking his heart."

I flinched knowing he was right. "I doubt I broke his heart, Ian," I said defensively. "He'll find someone else."

"You just don't get it, do you?" He said rubbing his forehead. "My brother really cares about you and you played him like a fool. I hope you're happy with whatever-his-name-is."

Averi had been quietly watching, letting this play out. Finally, she said, "Ian, I think she got your point." She grabbed him by the elbow and walked him out of earshot. I saw her talking quietly and he nodded, then turned and left. She walked back over to me and put her arm around my waist. "Kendall, I don't know what's going on but this is getting out of control. I know you're lying to me about what happened here tonight and I know what you're going to say…drop it or leave it alone but I'm really worried about you." I stood there silently, my head screaming, "TELL HER! TRUST HER!" But my gut was telling me that if I did, something bad was going to happen. She stood in front of me, her eyes sad. "Kendall, you've got yourself locked up. Is this how you want to be for the rest of your life? Think about that." Shaking her head, she took me by the hand. "Let's get you home."

She hung around for a while and after she'd gone, I went down to my store, grabbed a journal off the shelf and went back up to my apartment. Lying against the pillows, I took a pen and put it to the paper, making swirls and squiggles then finally started to write until sleep finally took me.

The next morning, I was getting ready to go down when I heard the doorbell. As I opened the door, I was shoved back by Logan. He shut the door behind him and locked it. "I think it's time to finish what we started," he said grabbing my wrist tightly. He was pulling me toward him when I heard a knock on the window. Startled, he let me go and we both saw Averi with her face up against the glass.

"Let me in, Kendall! I need my coffee!" She said still knocking.

"Your friend is a pain in my ass," Logan growled as he unlocked the door allowing Averi to rush in.

She looked Logan up and down. "Well, hello there. What are you doing here?"

He glanced back at me and growled, "Not that it's any of your business, but I just stopped by to get some coffee."

She looked at his empty hands and a puzzled look came over her face. "I don't see any coffee…I would think you'd be drinking a protein shake from the looks of you. What the hell have you been doing? You've gotten really freakish looking."

Inside, I groaned. Averi never did have a filter. This was not the guy to insult. She was right, however. His biceps looked like they'd grown since the last time I'd seen him when he'd had me pinned against the wall. In true Averi fashion, she didn't let it go. "I'd suggest you lay off the 'roids or whatever you're doing. They say it makes your junk smaller." She looked down deliberately.

His nostrils flared and he bowed out his chest. "I don't do anything but natural stuff. The rest is just dedication in the gym, baby," he said stepping toward her menacingly.

Bravely, my pint sized hero stepped toward him. "You don't scare me you big ass! You've always had a chip on your shoulder and I can tell that as your shoulder got bigger so did the chip…unfortunately, your brain and junk only got smaller."

Just then, the door opened and George and Becky walked in. From the eerie silence, it was obvious the situation they'd walked into was a tense one. George, clearly sensing there was danger, cleared his throat and taking his cane, began to tap it in his hand like a baton. Glancing at each of us and seeing he was now outnumbered, Logan backed up and with a sneer, roughly pushed by George and went out the door.

George and Becky stood staring at Averi and me with their mouths open. "What the heck was that?" George asked looking out the door to make sure Logan was gone. When he was satisfied he was out of sight, he turned back for an explanation. "Well?"

Averi stepped forward, hands on her hips. "That roidhead was in here manhandling Kendall!" She said glaring at me as I absently rubbed my wrist. "I don't know what he would've done if I hadn't showed up early." She now faced me and I knew it was coming. "What the hell was going on?"

Again, I knew the right thing was to tell her and not face this alone but Sebastian's voice was ringing in my head. If I told about Logan, it would lead to Sebastian and I just couldn't afford to have that happen.

I laughed nervously. "Nothing was going on, he was just coming by to offer me a pass to the gym he works in. You know, a trial membership?"

Averi scowled. "He had his hands on you, Kendall. Explain that away…again. And if that was the case, why was the door locked?"

"Well, um, he was showing me that they do self-defense classes, too," I said, thinking fast. "He was trying to make me break the hold but I couldn't. Guess I need to take the class," I said shrugging trying to keep a smile on my face even though I wanted to cry. "I must've locked the door out of habit when he came in."

George and Becky exchanged glances, and I knew this story was just too bogus for words, but I had to stick to it. "Anyway, I guess I'll look into those classes on my next day off." I walked over and started wiping tables and straightening the books on the shelves. You could hear a pin drop, and I knew they were all still staring at me, but I held my composure. Finally, shaking their heads, they went about their normal routines. Later that day, I was standing by the front picture window, and I saw a figure I knew immediately. It was Tristan. He walked down the steps to the beach, surfboard in hand and headed to the water. I felt tears welling in my eyes as the ache in my heart became a physical pain. He was so beautiful, and I noticed the girls walking down the beach turned as he walked by but he didn't even spare them a glance. He met up with Hoby and after a handshake, they paddled out into the surf. My heart was thundering in my chest, and I knew this must be how it felt for your heart to break into pieces. Sighing, I sat at the table and watched them bobbing in the waves until a swell came, and I saw Tristan paddling methodically until he popped up on the board. He was amazing to watch as he carved through the wave almost to the beach. When he wiped out, I held my breath until he surfaced and waved at Hoby to let him know he was okay. The rest of the afternoon, I managed to watch them a few times until I saw the waves had calmed and they were walking up the beach together. Peering through the blinds, I watched as they shook hands and Hoby headed down the beach as Tristan came toward the boardwalk. He appeared to be deep in thought making his way through the thick sand close to the pier when suddenly he looked directly at my store. It was as if he could see me, but I knew that wasn't possible. He stopped and stood watching for a few minutes then, shaking his head, walked out of my sight. My bottom lip started quivering as my emotions welled up and the tears stung my eyes.

Someone cleared their throat behind me and taking a deep breath and blinking back the tears, I turned to see George standing right behind me. "Kendall. It's none of my business and you can call me a nosy old man, but I can see you've got it bad for that young man and something's definitely keeping you from being with him…from being happy."

I turned back to gaze at the darkening sky. "George, it's complicated."

He placed his hand on my shoulder giving it a gentle squeeze. "I met my wife when I was about your age. She was a bright young woman with a smile that could light up a room. I saw her and instantly knew she was the one. There were a lot of things standing in our way but I said to myself, 'George, do you want to look back in fifty years with regret or do you want to look back with a lifetime of beautiful memories?' I took the beautiful memories and thank God for every day I had with her." I took a hitching breath trying to keep my composure. "Kendall, you deserve a lifetime of happiness. Don't let the one you love slip through your fingers."

Biting my lip to stop it from quivering, I turned and gave him a sad smile. "George, you don't know everything about me, and if you did, you wouldn't say that." I eased myself from his grip and walked away.

A week had passed without incident, George had backed off and then I got the surprise of my life. The bell on the door chimed as it opened and I glanced up as I was ringing up a sale. My mouth fell open as I saw Ian walk in, glance around the store, then find a seat. I cautiously approached and when he saw me, he smiled. "Good morning, Kendall. I'd like coffee, please."

"Okay…do you know what you want?" I said, pointing up at the menu board, still disbelieving he was here.

"Um, I don't care," he said looking around at the bookshelves. "Wow, you have books here, cool."

I held my order pad in front of my mouth to hide my smile. "Yeah, we *are* a bookstore."

He nodded, still looking around. "Well, I'd like coffee and I might just buy a book." I looked at him incredulously wondering what had possessed him to come in, but my thoughts were interrupted by another customer coming in.

"I'll be right back," I said as he checked his phone and began to text. I brought his coffee and the cream and sugar to the table. "How do you like it?"

He looked at me puzzled. "I don't know, I haven't tried it yet."

"I mean, how do you want it? Cream, sugar?" I was starting to wonder if he'd ever had coffee before.

"Oh, um…how do most people drink it?" Now, I *knew* he hadn't had it before.

I took the creamer and held it over his cup. "I'll take care of it." I put a splash of cream in and a couple of sugars and left him to stir it. He seemed totally fascinated by the coffee and I had to laugh. When he took a sip, he smiled brightly. He mouthed, *this is good!*

It was funny at first but after three hours of him sitting there, I wasn't laughing anymore. "Ian, don't you have somewhere to be?" I asked as I brought him his fifth coffee, this one iced with whipped cream and caramel on top.

"Nope, and I believe since I'm a paying customer, you can't throw me out, right?" He asked grinning as he waved his money at me.

I shook my head and rolled my eyes. "No, I can't throw you out. And you're even wearing a shirt and shoes. But surely, there's got to be a beach bunny with your name tattooed on her, just waiting for you."

He looked up at me with a hurt expression on his face, his lips pouting. "Why are you being mean to me? I don't have any beach bunnies anymore. I'm saving myself for someone special. I'm changing my ways."

My eyes grew wide and my mouth fell open. He actually sounded sincere. "Hey, I'm sorry," I said setting his coffee down. "I know you probably don't have a lot of respect for me right now because of what happened with Tristan and I have no right to be mean to you. You're not involved."

Taking a sip from his coffee, he smiled showing me his whipped cream mustache. "I have nothing against you, Kendall. That's between you and Tristan. But I will say this, he's the best guy you'll ever find. I can promise you that." He got up from the table and walked over to the bookshelves. "So, my mom likes to read, can you pick out a book for me to give her?" He ran his finger over the spines of the books. "Just don't pick that shades of whatever book. I don't want to know if my mom would read that."

I laughed out loud. "Oh Ian, you're killing me!" I picked up a romance book that Katie had on her wish list and handed it to him. "Here, this is one your mom wants."

He looked at the half-naked model on the cover and shook his head disapprovingly. "My mom reads this? Good grief. What is it with you women?"

"We love romance. That's it in a nutshell. If you plan on winning the heart of your someone special, you may want to read one of these." I patted him on the shoulder and left him flipping through the book.

Ian stayed the rest of the day. He drank more coffee than was humanly possible, texted constantly, flipped through the magazines I had scattered around for the customers and eventually bought the book for his mom. By the end of the day, he'd kinda grown on me. As I was ringing up his purchase, he sheepishly grinned. "I bet you're ready for me to get out of your hair, huh?"

I looked at him and genuinely smiled. "No, actually, this was the first time I actually got to see the real you and I have to say, you're nothing like I expected. I can see you making someone very happy one day." I slid the book into a bag along with a pretty bookmark as a gift for Katie. "Take care, Ian."

Taking the bag, and turning to leave, he stopped. "Kendall, I'm sorry for judging you, too. I just wanted to say that. Goodnight...And take care."

As he shut the door behind him, I turned the lock and leaned back against the door. The world really was full of surprises and this was definitely a big one.

Chapter 13

Tristan

Ever since the day Kendall sent that text, I hadn't been able to get her off my mind. I knew there had to be something going on but couldn't figure out what. My mom had been very supportive despite her own grief and we'd spent a lot of time together talking over what had happened and couldn't come up with any reasons. I rarely saw Ian except in passing at work and when he wasn't at work, I'd see him hanging around near the boardwalk when I was surfing. To keep myself busy, I also filled my time with work and squeezed in some surfing to try to clear my mind. It didn't help. From the beach, I could see her store and longed for a glimpse but never saw her. I kept hoping that she'd call me and tell me she'd made a mistake and I'd be on my way to sweep her into my arms and never let go. She never left my mind even for a second. I was at work with a million things to do and was sitting in my office doodling Kendall's name on a scrap piece of paper. My daydreams were interrupted when Jerica buzzed me. "Mr. O'Neal? There's someone here to see you." She lowered her voice to a whisper, "She's got purple hair."

Instantly, I knew who that was. Laughing, I said, "Send her in!"

The door opened and Averi came in glaring back at Jerica. "Haven't you ever seen purple hair before? Geez!" She shut the door behind her and sat down in the chair across from me. Her eyes glanced to the notepad full of doodles and I saw a faint smile. "Tristan, I'm sorry to bother you at work but we need to talk."

Quickly scooting the paper into a drawer, I leaned back in my chair. "It's not a problem, what's up?"

She fidgeted in the chair, looking around my office, then began. "I have a theory about what's going on with Kendall and I need your help because I think she's in danger." She seemed to be totally serious.

Giving her my full attention, I leaned my arms on the desk. "Go on."

"Okay, I started noticing that a couple of guys, Sebastian Cole and Logan Walker have been pretty much become permanent fixtures on the boardwalk the past week or so. I don't think you know who Sebastian is but let me tell you, he's a real creep. He used to hang around with Kendall years ago before her family passed away. I've never liked him. Logan is a jock wannabe who I caught manhandling Kendall the other day. I needed help so I asked your brother to keep an eye on her by hanging out in the store and both creeps conveniently disappeared."

"Whoa, wait…what do you mean manhandling? And my brother knew about this? Ian never said anything to me!"

"I asked him not to until I spoke to you. You see, Kendall got hurt not long ago. As a matter of fact, it happened sometime right after she broke up with you. A busted lip, bruises around her throat…she explained it away as clumsiness but I didn't believe her."

I could feel my face flush with anger. "Are you telling me someone laid their hands on her?"

She ran her hand over her face. "I'm embarrassed to tell you this…I thought it was you at first…and I'm sorry. But she told me right away that you would never hurt her and I believed her. I should've told you sooner but I…I wasn't sure if it was Sebastian or Logan but in my heart I believe it was one of them. I don't have any proof…and Kendall's not talking. I found out from Ian that she'd broken up with you and started to put two and two together."

I was so angry and disgusted that I slammed my hand on the desk. "I'll find whoever hurt her and I swear they'll pay."

Averi stood and put her hand on my arm. "Tristan, I feel the same way you do. We need to figure out what's going on and stop anything bad from happening to her but we have to have a plan."

I clenched and unclenched my fists then took a deep breath. "You're right. What do we need to do?"

She thought for a moment then said, "You need to come by my shop tomorrow and we'll talk more. I have a feeling something is going to happen…soon. Logan will be back, I just know it. He wasn't real happy when I interrupted him the other day."

"You caught him with her? What was he doing?"

"He had her in a wrist lock and when I knocked on the door, he snatched open the door and practically bit my head off. Kendall lied right to my face and told me he was talking about self-defense classes at his gym but I could see the fear in her eyes."

"Averi, I'll be there in the morning. You can count on it."

After a sleepless night, I went to the henna shop the next morning where I found Ian waiting with Averi. It was obvious they were in the middle of an argument when I walked in but since Averi was smiling, I figured she was harassing him. "How exactly do you think I'm being mean?" She was saying with her hand on her hip.

He looked surprised. "Seriously? Uh, well, you said the other day in front of some friends of mine that you wanted me to go sit in the bookstore even though you know I can't read. That was just mean!"

She laughed shaking her head. "I didn't say it like that, did I?"

He nodded emphatically. "Yeah! And then you said that I could find a book with pictures to keep me occupied." He looked truly insulted. "I can read! I did graduate, you know!"

"Okay, okay…but you know nowadays, graduating doesn't guarantee you can read. I'm sorry," she said smiling. "I hope I didn't ruin any chance you had with the beach bunnies you were with."

I stood watching them for a few moments and actually felt sorry for my brother. It was obvious he had it bad for her and that she had no interest in him. He glanced over at me as I walked up. "Tristan! Tell her I'm not as dumb as she thinks I am!"

I shook my head laughing. "He's not. Actually, he works with me at the bank now and from what his boss said, he's doing really well." I slapped Ian on the shoulder.

"Really?" Averi asked, eyebrows raised. "You have a job? At a bank? They let you work with money?" She sounded incredulous, and I could see Ian's face fall.

His mouth opened to respond when I heard shouting. "Hey you two, stop it. Listen." As we became silent, we could hear raised voices coming through the wall from the coffee shop. "Averi, is Kendall open yet?"

Looking at the clock she said, "She would have just opened!"

We listened closely and could hear Kendall speaking and a man's voice shouting. "I'm going over there," I said heading for the door.

"We're right behind you," Ian and Averi said simultaneously.

We rounded the front of her store and I threw open the door to find a man holding Kendall by the throat. "Logan, ple—" she gasped. Ah, this was Logan, one of the lowlifes we were expecting and a strong suspect in her assault. Grabbing him around the neck in a chokehold with my forearm, I felt him let go of Kendall. Gasping for air, she rushed toward Averi.

"Averi, call the cops! And get her out of here," I shouted as Logan tried to pry my arm from around his throat. Changing tactics, he got some leverage with his elbow, hitting me in the stomach. As the air whooshed from my lungs, I struggled to hang on, but I lost my grip. He spun to face me, balling up his fist to take a swing, but I ducked low and hit him in the abdomen. Taking him to the floor while he was still disoriented, I flipped him face down. Logan was still trying to fight, but I had the advantage keeping his arm behind his back. He was writhing and kicking but as soon as Ian grabbed his legs, he stopped struggling, his breath ragged and labored.

I heard Kendall shout, "No cops!" I looked over at Kendall and heard her plead, "Please, don't call them. It will only make things worse."

I shook my head at Averi and saw her end the call. She took Kendall by the arm and pulled her out the door.

Logan started to struggle again so I tightened my grip on his arm. "You move and you'll end up with something broken. Got it?"

He nodded slightly, his cheek smashed into the cold tile floor. "Yeah," he whined. "Dude, you guys are hurting me!"

I ground his face further into the floor. "Hurting you? What about what you've done to Kendall, you ass!"

"Ow! I didn't hurt her…I don't know what you're talking about," he whimpered. Ian and I exchanged glances and I twisted his arm further behind his back.

"STOP! You're gonna break my shoulder!" He squealed. "Okay, okay! I did it! I roughed her up but it was for Sebastian! He's the one you need to hurt!"

I never relaxed the tension on his arm and I could see his shoulder was close to popping out of the socket. "Logan, my brother is strong and not going to let go until you tell us everything you know. It's time to spill," Ian said angrily.

Sweat was popping out on Logan's forehead and he looked close to passing out. Finally, he gasped, "I'll tell you what I know."

Ian and I both hesitated to make him suffer just a few moments longer then eased up a little but kept him under our control. "Okay, spill," I said firmly.

He was still gasping, his eyes looking around wildly. "I still can't breathe," he rasped.

Ian looked at him and laughed. "If you can talk, you can breathe. Now, like my brother said, spill!"

"Okay, okay! Sebastian has something he's holding over Kendall." He took a ragged breath. "I don't know what it is but she does whatever he tells her to do to keep it a secret."

Ian glanced at me with narrowed eyes. "So, what's your role in this? Remember, we'll eventually ask Kendall so you'd better be up front with us," he said tightening his grip on his legs to emphasize our position.

He groaned and started whimpering, all the fight leaving him. "I delivered Sebastian's message. He ordered her to break up with you." My eyes snapped up to meet Ian's and we both nodded. I knew in my heart it hadn't been the Kendall I knew who'd broken up with me and now that had just been confirmed giving me hope that we still might still have a chance.

"And her injuries? Did you cause those?" I growled.

He swallowed hard and rasped out, "Yes…I did it. I wanted her and she wouldn't give me the time of day. I tried to…take what I wanted…" His words drifted away, his confession ringing in my ears.

I leaned in close to his face. "You listen and you listen good. If you touch her, look at her or even breathe in her direction again, we'll finish this and it won't be pretty. Do you understand?"

He hesitated, and I tightened up the grip on his arm. "Yes!" He groaned, tears flowing from his eyes. "I understand!"

As I was about to let him go, I slammed my fist into his jaw. "That's for Kendall, asshole."

Ian released his hold and I let go at the same time. He lay on the floor crying and clutching his shoulder as we both stood over him. "You're pathetic," I said shaking my head. "Get your sorry ass out of this place and don't ever, ever come near Kendall again. I mean it."

He struggled to his feet and holding his shoulder, he turned and ran from the store.

"So, bro! That was some major ass-kicking!" Ian said slapping me on the back. "Do you think he's stupid enough to try to come back?"

"I hope not, but if he does, he'll regret it." I looked around and saw Kendall at the door with Averi by her side.

With tear-stained cheeks, she looked at me and mouthed, *I'm sorry* before covering her face with her hands as she sobbed. Averi protectively put her arm around her as she motioned to me with her eyes to come over to Kendall. I walked over and touched her arm. She dropped her hands from her face and her eyes came up to meet mine. "Tristan, I'm just so sorry," she said, her chin trembling.

I pulled her into my arms and felt her relax against me laying her head against my chest. "Kendall, it's time," I said resting my cheek against the top of her head. "I need you to trust me and tell me what's going on."

She lifted her head from my chest and gazed into my eyes. "I will." The bell on the door jingled interrupting us. It was an older man I assumed was George. His eyes registered surprise when he saw me but he said nothing, just gave me a smile and went to sit at a table by the window. "Come back tonight when I close," she softly said, looking at each of us. "I promise I'll tell you everything then."

Reluctantly, I let her go but before I left, I gave her a gentle kiss on the forehead. "We'll be back around seven." She nodded with tear filled eyes. I took her hand, pressed it to my lips and let her hand slip from mine. My eyes never left hers as I followed Averi and Ian out the door.

Once outside, I stopped them and said, "I don't think we've seen the last of Logan. I think I should hang out at Averi's for a little while, just in case there's trouble."

Ian spoke up. "I think I should be the one to hang around. You need to stay away from here in case Sebastian's watching her. I have a feeling Logan won't be coming back today. His ego's too wounded…and his shoulder too for that matter. You sure put a hurtin' on that dude."

I studied my brother's face. "Are you sure that's the *only* reason you want to stay at Averi's today?"

His face contorted the way I knew it would when he was trying to hide a lie. His lips would try to curl into a smile as he tried to keep a straight face. "Uh, yeah. Why else?"

"Gosh, I don't know. Just asking," I said snickering.

"What's so funny? I just want to watch out for Kendall." The lips curled again and I couldn't help it, I burst out laughing.

"Okay, okay. I believe you! Call me if you see anything suspicious. I'll be over at mom's…it's close in case you need me."

As I walked away, I glanced back hoping that tonight, Kendall would finally share her secrets.

Chapter 14

Kendall

As the day came to a close, the butterflies in my stomach grew stronger. I knew it was time to share what I'd kept hidden for so long because it was obvious that I was dealing with two very dangerous, deranged people. Perhaps, if I finally shared this burden with someone else, if something bad did happen to me, at least someone would know the truth. I was sitting in my apartment and when a song came on the radio that seemed to be a sign. The words from "Brave" by Sara Bareilles seemed directed right at me. It was as if my family was sending me a message, and I sat in stunned silence listening to the words with tears rolling down my cheeks. I immediately downloaded it to my iPod and listened to it over and over, feeling the strength of my family flowing into me.

At precisely seven my doorbell rang, and I dashed downstairs. I unlocked the door to allow Averi and Tristan to file in. "Ian didn't come?"

Averi shook her head. "He thought you might be more comfortable telling just Tristan and me." My respect for Ian jumped again. They followed me upstairs to my apartment and both found a seat. I couldn't postpone it any longer. I paced in front of them, wringing my hands, trying to find the words to start. I reached over to pick up the picture of my family and holding it in my trembling hands, took a deep breath. "To tell you why I'm being harassed by Sebastian and Logan, I have to go back to the beginning."

Neither one spoke, they just listened. I heard my voice, shaky at first, become stronger with each word. I closed my eyes and felt myself going back in time to the first time I saw Sebastian.

"It was the second semester of eleventh grade when I met Sebastian and I had just been disciplined by Mrs. Locke for what seemed like the hundredth time,. I'd seen him around school here and there but he became friends with some of the kids I hung around with. Of all the friends I had at the time, he became the best listener and we became very close. He shared that his parents were a lot like mine and we compared stories of how we were constantly disappointing them. We became inseparable but I didn't intend to get caught up in a bad crowd, it just happened. Some of the guys started experimenting with drugs and I was pushed into trying them. I did it only once and after feeling like I was going to throw up, I totally regretted it. After seeing my reaction, they were cool with me not joining in but I was expected to help them with their buys and that's when the trouble really began.

I can remember that night like it was yesterday. We'd been hanging around in the pavilion most of the afternoon at Carolina Beach when someone suggested we go to the rocks at Ft. Fisher to watch the waves and chill. We snuck into the park just before dark and kept a low profile until we saw the last of the tourists leaving. After we'd been there for about an hour, several of them wanted to leave because they ran out of weed leaving only Sebastian, myself and one other guy named Charlie Maxwell. Charlie had been smoking weed all day and was pretty wasted. He was playing around, jumping from rock to rock while Sebastian and I sat watching. He was so high and I kept trying to get him to stop…I was afraid he'd get hurt. Sebastian was sitting beside me laughing, egging him on, telling me to chill out. Out of nowhere, Sebastian tried to kiss me. Instinctively, I pushed him away completely surprised. He'd never shown that kind of interest in me. He said, 'Kendall, I thought you knew how I felt. Don't you feel anything for me?' His expression was so pained and I remember saying, 'I don't want to hurt your feelings but no…I've always thought of you as a good friend.' He got angry and started swearing, shouting at the wind. I felt so bad for having hurt him and tried to talk to him but he was out of control. Out of the corner of my eye, I saw Charlie step toward the rock beside Sebastian and as he got there, Sebastian angrily pushed him. I honestly don't think he meant to hurt him but in the next instant, I saw his arms pinwheeling as he lost his balance and started to fall. Sebastian frantically tried to grab onto his shirt but it just slipped through his fingers. As he tumbled out of sight, I heard a thud followed by a splash. It was totally dark now and no matter how hard we tried, we couldn't see him. I screamed and screamed his name but he was gone."

I choked back a sob as my story continued. "Sebastian dragged me away screaming back to the car. I was hysterically crying and he threw me in the car. Once inside, he grabbed me forcing me to look at him and said, 'Kendall, you have to stop crying. We need to get our story straight.' Confused, I asked him what he meant and he explained that since nobody knew what happened, we would just leave and everyone would assume he was out there by himself, fell and drowned. Tearfully, I begged him not to lie. I told him I just couldn't do it! He then told me that if I didn't keep my mouth shut he'd make me pay." I glanced down at the picture in my hands and tears welled in my eyes blurring their faces. "I was so scared that I agreed but now I wish I'd never done it."

Taking a deep breath and wiping my eyes, I kept going. "Well, Sebastian drove me home, the entire time going over the story we were going to tell. When I walked in the house, my parents could tell something was wrong. Naturally, they asked where I'd been and I lied, telling them I'd gone down to the boardwalk with

Sebastian to keep up with our cover story. They accused me of sleeping with him and because I was so upset and sick over what happened that night, I never said any different choosing silence instead. I dashed to my room, locked the door and cried myself to sleep. The next day, Charlie's family reported him missing and a fisherman found his body later that afternoon. Immediately, all of my friends started calling and texting to tell me. The chain of lies had begun but inside I was dying because I knew the truth and wasn't able to tell anyone. A few days later, a police officer showed up at the house to question me since I was one of Charlie's friends and had been one of the last people seen with him. I panicked wondering if they'd talked to Sebastian and if he'd told them anything but when I opened my mouth, the lies we'd gone over came rolling out with no difficulty. The officer seemed satisfied and after he left, Sebastian called me. He made me tell him *exactly* what I'd said and seemed relieved that I'd kept my mouth shut. He still seemed a little paranoid about me telling my parents but I assured him that I wouldn't tell anyone. At the memorial service, Charlie's family was sobbing in the front of the church and my heart broke in two. I wanted so badly to run up to them and tell them the truth but Sebastian was sitting two rows behind me and I could feel his eyes boring into the back of my head. Two weeks later, another police officer and a detective came by the house because during Charlie's autopsy, they'd found drugs in his system and they wanted to see if I had any information on whom he would've gotten them from. My parents were sitting in during the interview since I was a minor and at the mention of drugs, my dad had gone ballistic. I'd never seen him so mad! Scared to death, I admitted that I'd only tried it once and never done it again. I was so scared! I told the officer that I didn't know the guy's name but knew where he usually hung out. After they left, my dad grounded me for a month and I ran upstairs to my room in tears. Not long after they'd left, Sebastian called me. He was totally freaking out! He'd heard the cops were at my house and wanted to know what that was all about. I told him why they'd come and what I said but he was totally paranoid and kept accusing me of telling the cops the truth. Over and over, I assured him I didn't but he kept on and on. He yelled at me that I'd pay for snitching and to watch my back. Honestly, it wasn't the Sebastian I knew. After I heard my family go to bed, I opened my bedroom window, crawled down the trellis and left the house intending to find him and tell him in person so he'd see I wasn't lying." My eyes fluttered open as I felt Tristan's arms wrap around me.

My heart pounding, I continued my story knowing this was going to be the hardest part to tell. "He wasn't home when I got there and I searched all the places we usually hung out until finally I gave up. I was making my way through the woods back home when I heard the sirens and smelled the smoke." I closed my eyes again as the memories of that horrible night overwhelmed me. "I started running praying it wasn't my house but when I came to the edge of the woods, the entire upstairs was engulfed in flames. The bedroom windows were shattering from the heat and smoke was pouring from under the roof. Firetrucks were parked all over the yard and the firefighters were aiming the huge jets of water at the flames but they didn't seem to be making a difference at all. As I got closer, I could see a crowd had gathered on the sidewalk and I searched frantically for my family among the sea of faces but couldn't see them. I just knew they had to still be inside so I started screaming for someone to help them. Everyone was so busy fighting the fire so I tried to run in the back door but on my way up the steps, a firefighter grabbed me. The heat was intense and debris was falling as the fire spread throughout the lower floor. He pulled me out of danger but I fought him…I had to save them! I could picture them afraid and trying to get out. Kicking and screaming until I broke free of his grip, I dashed to the door but another firefighter grabbed me. Exhausted, I couldn't fight anymore. I collapsed in his arms and right before I blacked out, the last thing I saw was my house collapse in on itself. I regained consciousness screaming in the back of an ambulance on the way to the hospital. They gave me sedatives to calm me down but all I could do was ask if my family was okay. Nobody wanted to tell me anything. After a few hours, they had a hospital chaplain come in to tell me they hadn't made it out. I became hysterical again and begged them to call my best friend and thank God, Averi, you didn't turn me away." I opened my tear-filled eyes to see Averi giving me the most loving smile. Tristan rubbed my back in a soothing circular motion. "Go on, Kendall. We're here for you."

Just being with them gave me strength. "The next day, my grandparents came to make all the arrangements," I continued, "and they begged me to go with them to their farm but I just couldn't bring myself to go. Two days later, we had the memorial service for my family and I can honestly say, I barely remember that day. I do remember the high school sent a beautiful wreath of lilies for Kelsey…they were her favorite. Except for the picture I have, there were no family pictures left so friends and family had gotten together and made a collage of their memories of my family. During the service, I felt so numb watching person after person walk up to talk about how wonderful my family had been and how God had gained new angels. When I heard the last comment, I wanted to jump up and scream, "NO! I want them here!" But I stayed mutely in my seat, clutching my grandparents' hands. At the visitation, we walked to the reception room and I shook hands with hundreds of friends of the family who all told me wonderful stories but each anecdote was like a knife in my heart. All I could give in response was, "Thank you for coming." My grandmother, sensing I'd just about had enough, whispered for me to take a break. I dashed away to a quiet room in the back of the church to gather my thoughts. I grabbed some tissues and was trying to stop the flow of tears when I heard the door open. I looked up to find Sebastian standing at the door. I'd asked where he'd been and explained how I'd tried to find him to tell him exactly what the cops had said. He'd stood staring at me, silently as if he still wasn't convinced. I'd promised him that I didn't tell them anything. I'd explained they'd told me they found drugs in Charlie's system and asked me if I knew any dealers. I told him I gave them a fake lead at the snow cone stand because I didn't want them to find out it was Colin who was dealing after stealing the drugs from his dad."

At the mention of Colin's name, Tristan seemed surprised. "Colin Burns? The guy whose dad is a doctor and he's now an EMT?"

"Yes," I answered. "Do you know him?"

He nodded slowly, a thoughtful look on his face, then said, "Yes, I do. Kendall, go on."

"Well, after I finished, he'd kept staring at me as if in a trance then grabbed me by the arms pulling me to him. From the look in his eyes, I'd been afraid he was going to try to kiss me again, but instead, he growled in my ear, 'You wouldn't want anyone else to suffer like your family did, would you Kendall? You'd better keep our secret.' I'd been stunned! I'd stared into his cold eyes and seen a stranger. He'd pushed me away and walked out. I knew I should tell someone what I suspected but the fear of retaliation kept me silent. Sebastian knew all about my life...It would have been so easy for him to find and hurt someone I loved. From then on, whenever I saw him, he'd always manage to remind me about our secret. The frequency of his visits got less and less until I figured he'd gotten bored with me. Unfortunately, he showed up again right around the time you and I started dating," I said sadly, my eyes meeting Tristan's. "The jealousy thing came raging out of him when he found out I was seeing you and the coward sent Logan to straighten me out." My voice cracked as the memory of Logan's visit came rushing back to me. "He'd shown up one morning before everyone else got here. He'd grabbed me from behind and threw me into the wall in the kitchen so hard it knocked the breath out of me. Then he grabbed my throat so tight I couldn't breathe. He'd told me he was delivering a message from Sebastian. The message had been to break up with you." My breath was coming out in short bursts and swallowing hard, I shook my head to try to make the memory of my terror go away. Tears leaked from my tightly closed eyes, and I felt a sob escape.

"Kendall, what did he do to you," Tristan said softly, pulling me close.

I lay my head against his strong chest and clenching my eyes tightly, I let it out. "After he gave me the message, he forced himself on me, kissed me…touched me…" I felt Tristan tense but silently, he held me tightly. "I was so afraid he wasn't going to stop and if George hadn't come in, I *know* he would've taken what he wanted."

"If I'd known this earlier, I'd have broken his damn neck," Tristan said through clenched teeth. He looked down at me and his eyes glistened with tears.

Averi stood, cleared her throat and I could tell she was fighting back tears. "I'm always going to be here for you, bestie. You're being so brave," she said before walking over to give me a tight hug. "I think I'm going to give you guys some privacy." She gave Tristan a hug too and walked to the door. As she opened it, she turned back and said with a sad smile, "I love you and I know you're going to be just fine."

As the door closed, I gazed up into Tristan's beautiful blue eyes. I softly touched his cheek and whispered, "I'm so sorry I didn't tell you…I'm just so tired of being afraid."

Brushing a strand of hair away from my face, he kissed me softly. "Kendall…I love you. Let me put a stop to this."

It took me a moment to absorb what he'd said. "You love me?" I asked as my heart soared.

He smiled while he nodded, "I was trying not to…I really was. It was tearing me apart not being able to see you or hold you. When you told me you were seeing someone else, my head told me to move on but my heart wouldn't listen. Baby, I do love you and I'm kinda hoping you feel the same way."

"Well, the truth is…I've loved you for a long time. Ever since you caught me in your arms in high school…but you wouldn't remember that."

He laughed and wrapped his arms around me as he dipped me into the exact position I'd fallen into that day. "As I recall, I asked if you were okay, helped you up and you ran off. What *you* didn't know was that I looked for you every day after that but I never saw you again."

I stared at him, disbelieving. "You looked for me? I was so embarrassed about what happened that I hid in the bathroom. After that day, I just watched you from the shadows. Plus, you were dating perfect Maria. You wouldn't have given someone like me a second look."

He gently cupped my face drawing my gaze upward to meet him eye to eye. "Kendall, you are the most beautiful woman I know, inside and out. You thought you were the one that fell that day all those years ago, but it was really me and I fell hard. For a while, all I could do was think about you but after searching the crowds in the hallway every day for months, I finally I gave up. The night of the bonfire, somehow I knew it was you. I had a familiar feeling inside and I knew I had to find out if it was the one person who made my heart skip a beat." He pulled my hand to his chest to rest it where his heart was beating rapidly. "I can't help it, it beats that way every time I think of you. My heart's all yours, if you want it…I don't want to spend another moment away from you."

Our lips came together, softly at first then more urgently, as we made up for the precious time we'd wasted. Wordlessly and never breaking eye contact, we slowly began to undress each other, the anticipation of seeing each other's bodies only building the desire. The cool air kissed my flushed skin as he slid his hands under my cotton t-shirt and lifted it over my head. As his hands slipped behind me, caressing my skin, I moaned, the sensation of his touch almost too much to bear. I tugged impatiently at his shirt and saw the corner of his mouth curl into a wicked smile. In one motion, he pulled it over his head and tossed it to the floor then pulled me closer. Seeing his tanned chest and perfectly sculpted abs, I licked my lips then kissed his collarbone working my way down, his muscles flexing at my touch. The vibration of a growl coming from his chest spurred me on as I explored the contours of his perfect body. Piece by piece, our clothes dropped or were thrown to the floor leaving nothing between us. Suddenly, Tristan swept me up into his arms as if I were as light as a feather and carried me over to the bed where he lay me gently onto the soft comforter, my hair fanning across the pillow. Climbing onto the bed, he slowly and deliberately grazed my bare skin with his fingertips, and I felt myself shuddering with desire as I arched toward his touch, needing and wanting more. As he gazed into my eyes, I wrapped my arms around his neck threading my fingers into his silky hair to pull him down for another searing kiss. My body felt as if it was on fire from his kisses alone.

"Oh baby," he moaned against my mouth. "I can't get enough of you." He tangled his hand into my hair tilting my head back to allow access to my neck. I willingly tilted my head and he gently sucked on my earlobe before feathering kisses down to my shoulder where he playfully nipped my skin sending intense shivers up my spine.

The brush of his beard gave me goosebumps, his scent intoxicated me. When his mouth found mine again, the kiss was more deliberate, more provocative. Our tongues tangled, the friction causing my body to tremble and I whimpered when I felt as if I were losing my breath. Every tender caress brought us closer. Our hearts began beating as one. We were physically crying out for each other and when joined, we united not only our bodies but our souls.

Chapter 15

Tristan

We lay tangled in the sheets. My arms wrapped around her. It was an amazing feeling to be back where I knew I belonged. We were together again, and I was going to do my damnedest to make sure we stayed that way. Her past was still haunting us and if Sebastian found out we were back together, Kendall was still in real danger and that worried me. I turned my head slightly to take in her beauty. By the light of the moon streaming through the window, I could see her absently tracing a heart on my chest as she lay in the crook of my arm. She turned her head slightly to look up at me. "I'm so happy right now," she sighed.

"Me too, baby," I said as I kissed her forehead.

She smiled but then furrowed her brows. She was sensing my tension. "Is everything okay?" When I just sighed, she lifted herself up on one elbow while resting her hand on my chest.

I rolled over on my side to face her and tucked a stray strand of hair behind her ear. "I love you and want to be with you but this secret is going to end up keeping that from happening."

She lay back onto the pillow and closed her eyes. "I just want this all to be over," she whispered. "What *can* I do?"

For starters, I was picturing Sebastian's ass being thrown in jail like on "Cops" but realistically, from Kendall's story, there was no real evidence of intent to kill. It was most likely her word against his about what happened that night and I doubted that would convict him. I also worried about what punishment Kendall would face for not telling the truth about what happened that night. I suspected he may have had a hand in the fire that claimed her family. The way she described his actions at the funeral, it sounded really suspicious.

"Honestly, Kendall, I think you need to confront him and baby, you won't be alone."

She sat straight up, eyes wide and shook her head. "He'll never say anything in front of you. If he even finds out we're together…"

I took her hand in mine pressing my lips gently to her fingers. "Baby, I'll be right there listening, he won't even know I'm there." It was risky and there was a strong possibility that he would flip out and do something stupid, but I had a plan and hoped it would work. "I want him to find out we're together. I think that'll be the one thing to draw him out."

Her bottom lip quivered. "Tristan, I'm so scared."

Pushing her back down to the pillow, I kissed her gently. "I swear I'll protect you. We have to put this thing with Sebastian to rest, one way or the other if we're ever going to have a future together."

Nodding, she cupped my cheek then softly said, "I know you're right." She kissed me gently. "Tristan, please don't leave me tonight."

With those few words, she had me. "There's nowhere else I'd rather be." Leaning toward her, I saw her lips part in anticipation allowing me to capture her luscious mouth once more with mine.

The next morning, I felt something tickling my nose and upon opening my eyes, found Kendall sitting beside me brushing her silky hair across my face. "Wakey, wakey," she giggled. Wrapping my arms around her, I wrestled her down onto the bed.

"Good morning, beautiful," I growled while kissing and nibbling her creamy skin. As I moved along her collarbone, she squirmed, and I remembered she was ticklish. I took advantage of this and nibbled along the ridge as she giggled and squealed trying desperately to fight me off. Breathless, she finally pleaded with me to stop, unable to stop the giggles. I relented and when I let her go, she pounced on me pushing me back onto the bed. Pouting her perfect full lips, she kissed me softly, her hair cascading down around my face in a mass of loose curls.

Our morning romp was interrupted by the doorbell and I cursed inwardly at the disruption. She dashed over to grab a robe and leaving the door open, went down to see who was downstairs. A moment later, she came dashing back in the door, the color drained from her face. "It's Sebastian!" She cried. "What are we going to do?"

This was the perfect opportunity to get him to talk. Either he knew I'd spent the night or if he didn't, it was definitely something I wanted him to know. "Kendall, I want you to go down and tell him you'll be right down. I then want you to go to the kitchen and prop open the back door." She was picking up clothing and after throwing some on, ending up with my t-shirt. As she started to pull it back off, I stopped her. "Wear that." When she gave me a puzzled look, I said, "He'll know it's mine and I'm getting ready to walk right by him. This should get things rolling."

"Tristan, what if he tries to hurt me?" She asked her eyes filled with fear.

I pulled on my jeans and slipped on my shoes. "You won't have to worry about a thing. I'll be coming in the back door and I'm calling Ian to have him meet me here." She quickly finished dressing and ran a brush through her hair. At the top of the stairs, I pulled her to me giving her a quick reassuring kiss. "It'll be okay. I promise."

We noisily descended the stairs and as I walked into the view of the front window, I could see him peering in the window. As he saw me, his face clouded over with anger. I deliberately gave Kendall a passionate kiss before unlocking the door. As I started out the door, Sebastian blocked me, so I stopped. "Excuse me," I said before shouldering by him while giving him an even glare.

I heard him call me an asshole under his breath as I walked away, but I didn't respond. Instead, I rounded the corner, running to the rear of the store to make my way back in through the back door. Ian came up just a moment later followed by Averi. I put my finger to my lips to keep them quiet and we silently and stealthily entered through the kitchen to the area right by the door. Luckily, the kitchen door was slightly ajar so we were able to hide but still were able to hear what was being said.

I could hear Sebastian's voice but it was very low. Kendall walked casually toward the kitchen, drawing him over to us and finally we could hear what he was saying.

"Logan came to me and told me he wasn't going to be helping me with you anymore. He had his arm in a sling and a swollen jaw…would you know anything about that?" He paused, eyebrows raised. "Now, I come to see what's going on and I find you've been with Tristan. I ordered you not to see him anymore," he hissed. I could see through the crack in the door that he was stalking back and forth, his jaw clenched as tightly as his fists. "You obviously don't care about your friends or family."

Kendall stayed calm and I was so proud of her. "Sebastian, you're not going to hurt the ones I love, I know you better than that. As for Tristan, I've always loved him and can't just stop because you tell me to." She kept backing closer to the kitchen and he followed without realizing what was happening.

His face was flushed with anger. "Why can't you love me? What's he got that I don't have?" He spat out.

With a gentle tone, she said, "He is the most perfect person I know. I thought I knew what love was the first time I saw him but now I feel a love that is even deeper. I'm happy to say that he loves me too. Sebastian, you've always claimed you love me but how can you love someone and hurt them so many times like you've hurt me?"

He stopped pacing for a moment appearing startled. "Hurt you? How have I hurt you?" He sounded incredulous.

She took a deep breath. "First of all, you made me lie to a family that was grieving for their son. It broke my heart to watch their pain at his funeral all the while knowing that you'd caused it and I'd helped cover it up." Her voice softened. "We should've told the truth. To this day, in my heart, I never believed you meant to hurt him."

His pacing slowed, and I saw his hands slowly relax. "I didn't…none of this was supposed to happen!" He ran his hand through his hair. "That night I wanted to be alone with you but Charlie decided to stay. It really ticked me off but he was so stoned I figured I'd go ahead and tell you how I felt. He wouldn't remember it to tell anyone anyway." He slumped into a chair and threw his head back while closing his eyes. "I'd popped a couple of Xanax I got from Colin to chill me down and give me the courage to finally tell you how I really felt. Charlie was driving me crazy and the more he jumped around, the more he bugged me." He stopped speaking, a tortured look on his face. "When you gave me the 'you're just a friend' speech it hit me like a brick." He jumped up from the chair and resumed his pacing, and I could see his hands were shaking. Ian was motioning for us to go in but I shook my head no, afraid we'd spook him and set him off. "I love you, Kendall!" He said in a pleading voice.

Kendall spoke softly, almost too low to hear. "Sebastian, I loved you, as a friend. I don't know who you are anymore. Ever since that night, my life has been a nightmare. I'm done. I just can't lie for the rest of my life."

He stopped and stared at her. "Have you told anyone?" He asked as he grew more agitated. "Have you told *him*?" His face was damp, sweat beading on his forehead. He grabbed Kendall by the arm as he yelled, "Have you?!" A moment later, as if he realized what he was doing, he let go. "I'm sorry…" He paced back and forth again, muttering to himself. Suddenly, he shook his head as if coming out of a daze. "You said I've hurt you more than once. What did you mean by that?"

Kendall took a deep breath. "Did you have anything to do with the fire?"

It was as if she'd slapped him. All the color drained from his face, and he stumbled back a couple of steps. "Wh…why would you ask me that?" His hands started visibly trembling. She didn't answer, just watched his reaction. His mouth worked wordlessly, and he grabbed his hair and a guttural moan erupted from his throat. "Kendall! It wasn't supposed to happen!"

Chapter 16

Kendall

With his words still ringing in my ears, I felt myself go numb. "What do you mean?" I heard myself ask.

He covered his eyes with the palms of his hands, but I could see tears streaming down his face. "I mean, it was an accident. I never meant for anyone to get hurt."

I fell back against the counter for support. "You started the fire? You…?"

He crumpled into a chair burying his face in his hands before he began to speak. "The cops came to my house after they left yours. They kept asking me the same questions, telling me they *knew* what really happened. I stuck with the story but in the back of my mind, all I could think was that you'd caved in and told them everything. My dad finally told them that if they didn't have any evidence to charge me with anything that they'd better leave. I went upstairs to my room and smoked some pot and the more I thought about what the cops had said the more paranoid I got. I managed to get out of my house without my dad seeing me. It was late when I got to your house and no lights were on except for one in your window. I knew you used to get out of your house by climbing out the window so I climbed up the trellis and when I got up there, I found your window was open and you weren't there. I thought about calling you but realized I'd left my phone at home when I rushed out so I lay on your bed and waited. About half an hour went by and I was getting restless so I lit a cigarette. After I lay back down on your bed I must've fallen asleep. The smell of smoke woke me and I realized your comforter was on fire. I panicked and climbed out of your window intending to call the fire department as soon as I got far enough away that they wouldn't think I had anything to do with it."

"Sebastian! How could you leave my family in there? Why didn't you wake them up?" I cried. The images of that night came rushing back like a tidal wave.

He dropped his hands and looked at me with red-rimmed eyes. "I was stupid. By the time I got to the nearest phone, I heard the fire trucks headed over there. I snuck back through the woods and saw the whole upper floor in flames. I blended in with the crowd gathered outside and when I saw you running across the yard screaming, I couldn't take it and I left." He covered his face again and began to sob.

With tears rolling down my cheeks and a myriad of emotions swirling through my mind, I watched someone who'd tortured me all these years crumble into a pathetic heap. All the fear that had kept me locked up suddenly transformed into anger as the reality of what really happened to my family hit me. I'd always suspected Sebastian's paranoia had driven him to harm my family to get to me but now I realized he'd been a stupid, scared kid who'd used the fire as leverage to keep me in his control. I wanted to scream but when I spoke, my voice was calm. "All this time, you had me scared to death that you'd do something to the people I loved if I didn't do as you wished. Do you even know what your pal Logan did to me? I think you should know what kind of degradation he put me through."

His head snapped up. "What do you mean?"

I glared at him, "He took your 'orders' to another level. He thought it was okay to slam me around and grope me all in your name. He also left me with a busted lip and bruises on my throat. Was that part of your intimidation plan?"

The disgusted expression on his face told me he hadn't known about Logan. "Kendall, I didn't know…he was just supposed to scare you. He was never supposed to hurt you or touch you."

"Well, he did and while we're on the subject, what about *you* under the boardwalk? Would *you* have taken it further if Averi and Ian hadn't shown up?" I asked angrily.

He dropped his head in shame. "All I wanted from the first moment I saw you was for you to love me," he said, his voice breaking. "I kept hoping you'd feel something for me. When Tristan came into your life, I knew I'd never have a chance. It kills me that you've been hurt." He sighed and dropped his head. "Go ahead and call the police now…to turn me in."

I wanted to, I really did but in my heart, I knew the law wouldn't fix this. I looked over to the kitchen and motioned for Tristan to come in which he did very slowly followed by Averi and Ian. Sebastian looked up and instead of anger, his face exuded only guilt and shame. Tristan took my hand, and I drew on his strength. "I'm not going to call the police. Since I know the truth about what happened with Charlie, I intend to go to his family and tell them exactly what happened that night. I want my conscience clear. As far as my family, their loss is something I'll never forgive you for but putting you in jail for an accidental fire won't bring them back." Sebastian lifted his eyes, a look of disbelief on his face. "The people in this room are the only ones who need to know what happened, but keep this in mind…they are my witnesses so the game is over."

Sebastian nodded, resignedly. "I'll leave town. I haven't got anything here for me anyway."

Tristan stepped in front of me, crossed his arms and said, "I think that's an excellent idea…"

I placed my hand on his back. "Tristan, let him go. I'm ready for this to be over and done," I said softly.

Sebastian got up and walked to the door, the silence in the room deafening. "Again, I'm sorry for everything, Kendall," he said before turning to walk out the door.

I felt Tristan's arms wrap around me, and I sank back against him. "Is it over?" I asked as tears slipped from my eyes.

He kissed my cheek then lay his alongside mine resting his head on my shoulder. "I believe so, baby."

Ian and Averi came into my view and I gave them a sad smile. "You ok?" Averi asked. With all the emotions running through me, all I could do was nod.

Throwing his arm around Averi's shoulders, Ian said, "Come on, Little Bit, let's give them some privacy. I'll buy you a snow cone." She rolled her eyes at him and lifted his arm off of her shoulder as if it were tainted.

"Will you stop calling me that?" She groaned before her mouth turned up into a grin. "And I want cherry!" She turned and dashed out the door laughing with Ian right on her heels.

Tristan smiled. "You know those two have it bad for each other, don't you?"

I had to laugh and said, "Yes, and that's no secret." I turned in his arms, slipped my arms around his waist and kissed him softly. "So, now that you know all my darkest secrets, are you still gonna stick around?"

His blue eyes sparkled as he brought his forehead to mine then he slowly went down on bended knee to take my hand in his. "Kendall, I'm glad I finally know about your past but now I want to focus on our future. There has always been a missing piece in my life and now that I've found you, I don't ever want to let you go. I'm not trying to rush you and I wasn't prepared with a ring, but when you're ready, I want you to know I love you and would be honored if someday you'd marry me."

For the first time in years, I was free of fear and my heart felt so light and full of love. I knelt down with him and pulled both of his hands to rest over my heart. "Tristan, you've had my heart from the first moment I saw you…it will beat only for you until the day I die. I love you and would love to marry you, any day." He leaned in and kissed me until I was breathless. Quickly standing, he pulled me to my feet, swept me into a bear hug and swung me around while smiling broadly. In one move, he cradled me in his arms against his bare chest and strode up the stairs, pushed open my apartment door and carried me to the bed where he dropped me onto the fluffy comforter.

"Let's finish what we started," he growled. My eyes took in his tanned sculpted chest, and I sat up to grab onto the taut muscles of his waist pulling him onto the bed. He tumbled down next to me but when I moved to kiss him, he shook his head and pushed me back down against the pillows. "I want to enjoy every inch of you," he said tucking his fingers under the hem of his oversized t-shirt to stroke my stomach lightly. My skin tingled with anticipation leaving me aching for more. My body was straining for him, but he calmed me with a kiss and a whisper to be patient. His slow exploration was making me want to scream and I bit my lip to keep myself still but inside, I was crying out for release. I found my breathing had quickened. My heart was racing. He tugged my shirt up, and I lifted myself to allow him to pull it over my head. His eyes raked over my white lacy bra, and he rasped, "God, Kendall, your body's so incredible." The sound of his voice along with his touch was setting me on fire. I felt myself shiver from the heat of his hands as they slipped my shorts down to my ankles where I seductively kicked them off right back onto my face. The flames of desire dampened slightly until I felt Tristan pulling them away from my eyes and I saw him smiling. "I love you, baby. That had to be the most precious thing ever." He kissed me softly then deepened the kiss as he threaded his hand through my hair pulling me against him. I couldn't resist touching his body any longer. My hands clutched his strong shoulders then I softly trailed my fingers down his back as he covered my body with his. He moved against me, the friction driving me insane until exasperated, I reached down and ripped the buttons of his jeans open. His eyes popped open in surprise, but I saw a mischievous smile tug at the corner of his mouth. "Somebody just can't wait, can they?" Instead of answering, I got to my knees and tugged his jeans down until they were completely off before tossing them onto the chair. He watched with a sly smile. He lay back with his hands behind his head and said, "Are you going to take advantage of me?"

I now had stripped him completely bare and smiling, I said, "Yes, for the first of many times." Standing beside the bed, I gave him a sultry smile and slowly peeled off my lacy bra while doing a sexy striptease. I could see his brows raise as I reached around to unhook it but turned away at the last moment then tossed it over my shoulder. When I glanced over my shoulder, I could see him swallowing hard before licking his lips. I made sure to shake my hips as I shimmied out of my panties and when I turned around, I found him standing right in front of me.

He took me by the hand, pulled me against him and said huskily, "Come to bed, baby. I can't wait any longer." With feverish intensity, Tristan and I gave in to our passion completely, body and soul.

Chapter17

Tristan

I drove up to the curb prepared to let her go by herself but she insisted I come with her. She took my hand and led me across the expanse of green lawn toward a huge elm tree casting its massive shadow, while the leaves rustling were the only sound. We stopped in front of the granite monument and Kendall knelt down to place the bouquet of lilies in the vase and prop a note against the cold stone. She brushed her fingers against the engraved letters, taking the time to trace every one. CHARLES and HELEN~BELOVED PARENTS and below it, KELSEY~TREASURED SISTER TO KENDALL were placed beneath the family name HART. Kendall looked up at me and smiled sadly. "Do you really think they know I made things right?" She asked.

I nodded and knelt beside her. "Of course I do. It took a lot of courage to face Charlie's family and tell them the truth." I put my arm around her shoulder and hugged her to me. Three months had passed since her confrontation with Sebastian. He hadn't been seen since.

She lay her head on my shoulder. "I still can't believe his parents were so gracious. Even after I told them what happened with Sebastian, they said they weren't going to ruin another young man's life by pursuing charges. I just hope he does something with his life to redeem himself for everything he's done. I'm also glad that the police finally busted Colin. He'd gotten away with selling drugs far too long." We spent a few more moments with her family then we stood and walked across the cemetery to pay our respects to my dad. My mom had picked black marble for his marker and had his picture engraved in the stone. As we held hands, I felt the diamond I'd given her pressing into my fingers and it made me smile. A butterfly fluttered by to land right on my dad's monument and Kendall turned to me and smiled. "I've heard that's a good sign."

Placing my hands on her cheeks, I gave her a gentle kiss. "I don't need a sign to know my dad approves…that was one of the last things we talked about. He could tell I loved you, even then."

We walked hand in hand back to my Jeep and as we drove away, she said softly, "I love you guys," as a tear ran down her cheek.

As we drove up to my mom's house, she came out the door waving. "Everything's all ready!" She grabbed Kendall by the hand and pulled her toward the house.

"Mom, you're gonna pull her arm out of the socket," I said laughing. I followed them inside to find the house beautifully decorated for the rehearsal dinner.

George greeted us first, followed by Becky and her husband. Although a traditional rehearsal dinner was just for the wedding party, my mom had posted an invitation in the store for all of Kendall's regular customers and several had actually come. She'd made me invite my co-workers and I had a few people show up. Kendall's grandparents had made the trip from their farm, and her grandfather was going to be giving her away.

Of course, Averi and Ian were there, albeit with tension so thick between them you could cut it with a knife. They'd been coolly civil to each other lately, but

I'd been waiting for the inevitable blow up. He'd been waiting patiently for her to come around but there were too many temptations, and he'd gotten busted by her out on a date one night and since then, she'd been dating Alex Reynolds, one of the local volunteer firemen. Ian had come whining to me about it, but he had no one but himself to blame. His heart belonged to Averi but his hormones hadn't quite gotten the message, and until he could grow up and stop chasing females, he had a snowball's chance in hell of getting anywhere with her.

The clinking of a glass got everyone's attention. "Hello, and welcome," my mom said smiling at everyone. "I want you to join me in celebrating the wedding tomorrow of my handsome son, Tristan to his lovely fiancée, Kendall." Everyone applauded along with a couple of whistles. "My husband Patrick may not be here with us today in person, but he's here with us in spirit and I know exactly what he'd say…may you have a lifetime of love and happiness. I love you both."

There were cheers and whistles and shouts of congratulations. George walked over and slapped me on the shoulder. "Well done, my boy. I'm glad you kids finally got together."

"Thanks, George. I am too." He handed me a beer, and we clinked our bottles.

Kendall came up beside me slipping her arm around my waist. "Can I borrow you for a minute?" She tugged me by the arm through the house and into my old bedroom where she shut the door. Pushing me up against it, she gave me a toe-curling kiss. Breaking the kiss, she smiled, her blue eyes dark with desire. "I just had to steal you for a moment," she said pressing herself against me. "You are just irresistible."

Cocking up an eyebrow, I shrugged. "I can't help it…it just comes natural."

She laughed and punched my shoulder. "You are so full of yourself." She kissed me again this time nibbling on my bottom lip. "I love you and can't wait for tomorrow. Oh, while I'm thinking about it, do you think Averi and Ian will behave tomorrow?"

I furrowed my brows as I thought about it, then said, "Who knows with those two. When I told Ian he'd be escorting her, he pitched a fit but I could tell he was gloating."

Kendall laughed. "I got the same reaction from Averi. She made it clear that her boyfriend would be coming but I honestly think he's just someone to make Ian jealous."

I growled, "Who cares what games those two play, I'm more interested in you." I pulled her to me threading my hand into her hair and was about to kiss her when suddenly a knock came at the door.

"Tristan? Kendall? Are you coming back out?" It was my mom.

I cleared my throat, "Yes, Mom. Be right out." Kendall giggled. "I was just showing Kendall my old room."

"Ok, dear. We're all waiting to go through the ceremony." I heard her walk away and I finished the kiss I'd started. She had a beautiful glow on her face as we walked out to join our friends for the rehearsal. We were doing the walk-through at my mom's but the actual ceremony was going to be on the beach. Kendall and Averi had done all the planning and my only role was to show up on the big day which was fine with me. Ian and I had been given white linen shirts and khaki pants to wear and given no indication of what my bride would be wearing or what colors she'd chosen. My mom had recruited her best friend Helen to be the wedding director and she gave us a quick rundown of the order of events. We were given our cues and told where to stand. We were following the old Southern tradition of having a stand-in for the bride during the rehearsal. Normally, when there were several attendants, the Maid of Honor would do the honors but since our wedding was small and Averi was the only bridesmaid, we had to find a volunteer. Luckily for us, a friend of mine agreed to fill in. Jane Anderson glided down the aisle on the arm of Kendall's grandfather and gave me a big cheesy smile when she finally stood beside me. Grinning, I whispered, "Thanks for doing this."

"No problem, Tristan…although the fact I'm obviously pregnant may have made some guests do a double take," she said under her breath. She gave me a wink as the minister began. We went through the entire ceremony and when Helen was satisfied we'd gotten everything right, it was time to eat some homemade barbeque and all the fixings.

Jay and Jane had arrived right before the rehearsal began, and I finally got to introduce them to Kendall. They hit it off right away and Jolene stood by shyly, so Kendall bent down to her level and asked her name. She blushed and giggled. "Jolene Marie," she said softly. "I'm gonna be a big sister."

Kendall glanced up to give me a wistful smile. "Jolene, there's nothing better than being a big sister. You make sure to give her lots of love, okay?"

She smiled, "I sure will. Her name's Olivia." She pointed to Jane's ample baby bump. "She's in my mommy's tummy but she's not ready to come out until her birthday."

Kendall held out her hand. "Well, Jolene…how'd you like to get some ice cream?" Jolene nodded vigorously and they walked away hand in hand.

We watched them walk away and Jane turned to me and smiled. "Tristan, she's beautiful. We're so happy for you and so glad you invited us to come. Callie and

Justin send their regrets but they are dealing with a cranky client as well as a sick baby."

Jay nodded, "Yeah, Ryder got some kind of virus and they didn't want to spread the bug. They told us to take lots of pictures and even gave Jolene a disposable camera of her own. Those pictures will be interesting, for sure."

I nodded in agreement. "Those will have to have their own album," I said laughing.

We joined the rest of the guests and every time I made my way over to Kendall, someone would stop my progress to congratulate me or reminisce about my dad. Finally, the guests started to leave, and I was able to pull her into my arms and hold her tight. "I can't wait for tomorrow. Are you sure you want to stay at Averi's?"

She nodded thoughtfully. "We need to finish some last minute details."

"Okay, baby. I love you and I'll see you on the beach." Cradling my cheek, she kissed me softly then walked over to meet up with Averi and with a glance over her shoulder and a wink, she was gone.

Chapter 18

Kendall

Averi and I had a blast the night before the wedding, drinking wine, making party favors and looking at her old pictures and yearbooks. As I found my tenth grade photo, I barely recognized the lost soul looking back at me from my picture, she seemed like a stranger to me now. Anxiously, I'd turned the pages to find Tristan's picture and had seen the same confident, handsome man I fell in love with all those years ago. It seemed unbelievable that I was about to marry the man of my dreams.

The day of the wedding started out with bright sunshine which was perfect for the beach setting. After a girl's morning to get our nails and toes done, Averi insisted on doing my hair for the wedding. She curled it into soft waves pulling it away from my face with pins and then accented it with a fresh lily. She was already dressed in her short one-shoulder fuchsia satin dress with sparkly flip-flops to match. She'd even added fuchsia highlights to her hair to match her dress. She helped me slip on my white satin strapless dress and deftly buttoned up the pearl buttons in the back. I needed her help to slip on my silver strapless sandals accented with rhinestones so I wouldn't damage my pedicure and then handed me my bouquet of stargazer lilies. My nana had charms made for my parents and my sister and had them mounted on a delicate chain that I wrapped around the base of my bouquet. When we were ready, we made our way down to the beach where my papa was waiting to escort me down the beach.

"Kendall, you look beautiful," he said holding out his arm for me which I took, giving him a gentle squeeze.

"Thanks, Papa. I'm so glad you and Nana could come. It means so much to Tristan and me," I said before giving him a kiss on the cheek.

Helen had set up a screen for us to stand behind until it was time for us to walk down the aisle. The music began provided by a friend of Averi's who played the violin and we watched as Averi walked out from behind the screen. At Helen's signal, Papa and I stepped out from behind the screen and I heard the murmurs of the guests as we made our way past them. I heard a tiny voice say, "She's marrying my prince!" I looked over to see Jolene waving wildly at me as I walked by. "Hi, Kendall!" She said with a huge smile. More smiles and even some tears greeted me as we walked by the guests but as soon as I my eyes met Tristan's they all faded away. He was smiling with his brows raised, and I saw him mouth the word *WOW*. The love shining from his eyes was so intense that I actually forgot to breathe for a moment. Tears were threatening to spill from my eyes, but I blinked them back trying to avoid raccoon eyes before the wedding even started. When we reached Tristan, he took my hand in his bringing me to his side. Smiling, the minister asked, "Who gives this woman to be wed?"

Papa had been practicing his one and only line and confidently said, "On behalf of our daughter, son-in-law and granddaughter, her grandmother and I do." He smiled and gave me a kiss on the cheek then went to sit with Nana who was dabbing her eyes with a tissue. I blew them both a kiss, turned to give Averi my bouquet then placed both of my hands in Tristan's. The minister began the service and as he was speaking, the one thought in my mind was that this had to be a dream.

We'd written our own vows so he began. Tristan smiled with tears glistening in his eyes. "Kendall, you are the one I've waited for all my life. You've brought me more love and happiness than I've ever known. Your beautiful smile, your limitless passion and compassion and your courage inspire me and make my life richer. I want to build a life with you, a family with you and grow old with you. You have my heart and always will…forever." Taking my ring from Ian, he lifted my hand, slid the ring on my finger then brought it to his lips kissing it softly before whispering, "I love you."

It took me a moment to compose myself before I spoke. "Tristan, from the moment I first saw you, I knew you were the one with whom I wanted to share my life. Your heart and mind inspire me to be the best person I can be. I promise to love you for eternity…to respect you, honor you, to be faithful to you, and to share my life with you and only you. I promise from the bottom of my heart, you have me forever." Averi handed me Tristan's ring which I slipped onto his finger.

The minister then repeated the question for Tristan. "Tristan, do you take this woman to have and to hold til death do you part?" He took my hands to his mouth and gave them a gentle kiss. Looking into my eyes, he answered, "I do!" I stood there mesmerized, lost in his eyes.

The minister got my attention when he asked, "Kendall, do you promise to love, honor and cherish Tristan as long as you both shall live?

My voice broke with emotion as I answered. "I definitely do!"

Tears spilled from my eyes freely because now I didn't care at all. My heart was bursting with love as I looked into those sparkling blue eyes. I vaguely heard the minister say, "You may kiss your bride," and felt Tristan's arms wrap around me and his lips move softly against mine. We heard a cough and broke apart to see our minister blushing before he introduced us to our friends and family as Mr. and Mrs. O'Neal for the first time.

I reached over to take Tristan's hand but instead, he scooped me up into his arms to carry me across the beach to the tents we had set up for the reception. Among the cheers and applause, I heard a squeal behind us and looked back to see Ian carrying Averi over his shoulder while walking to the party tent, her boyfriend was not far behind with a very unhappy look on his face. Tristan glanced over at his brother holding onto the now kicking and screaming Averi and laughed. "My brother's got it bad…let's just hope they don't kill each other before they realize they're meant for each other." He set me down when we entered our private tent that had been set up for us to change clothes in. Looking around to make sure we were all alone, he cradled my face in his hands, placed a gentle kiss on my mouth then brushed his lips across my forehead. "No more secrets, ever. Promise?"

Brushing his hair back with my fingertips, I gazed into the eyes of my true love knowing with him by my side, this was a promise I could definitely keep. With a big smile, I said, "I do."

The End….

Coming soon: The second in the Romance on the
Boardwalk series-

Chasing Rain